D0386348

BROTHER OF THE WOLVES

Weekly Reader Books presents

BROTHER OF THE WOLVES

BY JEAN THOMPSON
ILLUSTRATED BY STEVE MARCHESI

William Morrow and Company   New York   1978

This book is a presentation of
Weekly Reader Books.
Weekly Reader Books offers
book clubs for children from
preschool to young adulthood. All
quality hardcover books are selected
by a distinguished Weekly Reader
Selection Board.

For further information write to:
Weekly Reader Books
1250 Fairwood Ave.
Columbus, Ohio 43216

Copyright © 1978 by Jean Thompson
All rights reserved. No part of this book may be re-
produced or utilized in any form or by any means,
electronic or mechanical, including photocopying,
recording or by any information storage and retrieval
system, without permission in writing from the Pub-
lisher. Inquiries should be addressed to William Morrow
and Company, Inc., 105 Madison Ave., New York,
N.Y. 10016.

Library of Congress Cataloging in Publication Data
Thompson, Jean (date) Brother of the wolves.
Summary: An Indian boy, discovered in a wolf den
by a Sioux medicine man, struggles to win acceptance
into his adopted village.
[1. Dakota Indians—Fiction. 2. Indians of North
America—Fiction] I. Marchesi, Steve. II. Title.
PZ7.T371595Br. [Fic] 78-18014
ISBN 0-688-22168-8 ISBN 0-688-32168-2 lib. bdg.

Printed in the United States of America.

Acknowledgments and my thanks are due the following people who provided many helpful technical suggestions and comments: to Michael Lewis, Daniel R. Lynch, D.V.M., and Don Rickey, Western historian.

I'd like to add an extra word of appreciation to the Society of Children's Book Writers critique group, who contributed criticism and encouragement in equal measure, especially to Marie Halun Bloch and Laurie Gibb.

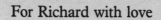

For Richard with love

BROTHER OF THE WOLVES

ONE

The mountain looked strong and solid, so firmly made of rock and earth it seemed impossible that any part of it could ever move. The solid look was only an illusion. The mountain was really soft and sliding, weakened by running waters that constantly gnawed like little silvery mice, nibbling away at the foundations.

An Indian man and woman moved slowly beneath the high wall of the mountain. They rode their horses along a narrow game trail, the man in front and the woman following behind. A baby in a cradleboard hung from the pommel of her saddle.

The warm spring sun shone down on the fresh, pale leaves and grasses. It was very still. Only one little bird made a small thin sound off in the trees.

Suddenly there was a deep grinding sound as the mountain groaned and shifted. Tons of rock and dirt broke loose on the slopes above the travelers. Booming and crashing, the mass roared down upon them. Before they had time to do more than raise their heads and look, they were gone. The horses were gone too, all lost and buried in the wild rush of the avalanche.

The rocks leaped and cracked as they plunged down the mountain. The dark, destructive earth spilled over, ripping out trees and bushes and carrying them along. The rumbling stopped. The hills again stood unmoving.

It was very quiet, as though the terrible thunder had never sounded. There was still one small thin cry, but it was not a bird. It was the baby. He was lying on top of a pile of dirt, and he was crying. He was all alone. He was the only one left, but he didn't know that. He only knew that he was afraid, that something strange and loud and sudden had happened, that something was very wrong.

He cried a long time, lying on his back on the ground. No one came to help him. The lack of attention made him angry and he cried harder, until he was tired. His cries turned to little hiccups, and then he went to sleep.

When he woke up, he forgot what had happened before. The sun was shining on him, and he felt warm and good. The wrappings of the cradleboard had been partially ripped away by the avalanche. He waved his arms and kicked his feet in the air, making happy little noises.

A wolf came out of the trees and walked across the rocks. Her gray fur was tipped with cream. Her tail was a creamy plume, and she had golden eyes. She padded carefully across the new raw rocks. They had not been there in the morning when she went down the game trail to hunt.

The breeze was blowing away from her, so she heard the baby sounds before she smelled him. She stopped, tipping her ears forward. She saw the little arms and legs waving in the air, and she wondered what he could be. She went down the slide to him.

He was very small. She sniffed at him and knew he was a baby by his milky smell. She whined and licked his face, feeling lonely and sad. Four pups had been born to her, but three had died. The den seemed very empty with only one puppy left.

The baby was happy to have someone come to see about him. He closed one tiny fist in the thick fur along the wolf's neck and gave a little whoop that sounded like a puppy bark.

The she-wolf licked him again and rolled him over with her nose. She gripped the wrapping skins with her teeth and picked him up, carrying him the way a mother cat carries her kittens. With her head high, she went across the fallen debris and into the trees.

The baby didn't cry. He hung limp and quiet in her jaws, his eyes half-closed and his bare feet dangling down. It was a long way to the wolf den, and he was heavy. The she-wolf put him down several times to rest. While she rested, she washed him with her tongue, cleaning off the dirt stuck on his skin. The baby liked this sensation and wiggled and cooed.

Her mate came out to meet her when they reached the den. He was larger and his fur was darker gray. She laid the baby down at his feet, and the male wolf smelled him carefully. He wagged his tail. The she-wolf picked up the baby and carried him into the den.

Gently she laid him down by her wolf cub and stretched out next to them. The wolf puppy at once scrambled to her and began to nurse. She nudged the human baby closer with her nose. He opened his mouth and drank too.

The wolves cared for him all that summer. He fed on wolf milk and, later, little bits of tender meat that he could chew. The wolf mother and wolf father washed him and slept close to him at night to keep him warm. He and his wolf sister wrestled and rolled around together on the floor of the den.

On nice days the wolves took them out into the sun to play. Wolf Mother lay quietly on the grass while the two babies romped and scrambled over her. When they became too rough or she was tired, she trotted off to a little hill and lay down alone. Then the two little ones, with happy yelps, jumped and bounced all over Wolf Father. They were good parents, and both babies were happy.

The long, warm summer passed. The green leaves were turning to brown and gold. The days were still sunny, but the nights were getting chill.

An Indian named Shadow Fox lay in the bushes across from the wolf den. He was perfectly still, and his buckskin clothes blended with the woods around him. The wind blew to him from the wolf den, and he knew they could not smell him.

He could see Wolf Father lying on the hill off to the side.

14

At last, Wolf Mother and a pup came out. The three wolves trotted away together. He knew the parents were going to give the little one a lesson in hunting.

Shadow Fox stood up and went to the entrance of the den. It had been a small cave in the rocky hillside. The wolves had dug it back farther, making it bigger and more protected.

Shadow Fox dropped to his knees and crawled inside. He was the medicine man for his Sioux village and had come to the wolf den for things to help give him power. He needed special objects—tufts of fur, bones, and teeth—to help him make his medicine.

The tunnel was narrow, and he squeezed around the curve on his hands and knees. It was dark inside and he couldn't see clearly. Suddenly he heard a strange sound coming from in front of him, and he realized he was not alone in the wolf den.

His heart gave a great leap in his chest. He jerked his long hunting knife out of his belt, turning the point toward the noise. Nothing happened. Slowly he eased to the side, drawing his body out of the opening. A little light came in, and his eyes adjusted to the semi-darkness.

Shadow Fox saw a human baby boy crouched on his hands and knees against the wall of the cave. He was naked and dirty and thin, and he was shivering with cold or fear. His lips were drawn back, showing a few baby teeth, and he was growling.

Shadow Fox sat quietly in the wolf den. He was surprised, but not as surprised as some people might have been. As a medicine man he knew that strange things happen. He understood that the wolves had somehow found the baby, adopted him, and kept him alive.

He also knew that the baby could not live through the winter. The mother wolf would lose her milk, and the baby could not live on raw meat alone. It would soon be cold, and without fur the baby would freeze to death. Game would be scarce, and the wolves must hunt farther and farther for food.

The baby could not run with the others and could not stay alone in the den.

Shadow Fox searched on the floor of the cave, picking up the things he had come to find. He put them in the pouch where he kept his charms and tied it to his belt. The baby watched him, growling now and then.

When he had gathered the things he needed, he picked up the baby. The baby growled and yelped, wriggling and struggling wildly, trying to bite him. Shadow Fox put him firmly under his arm and took him back to his village.

His people lived in a sheltered valley close to game and with good grazing for their horses. Water came from sparkling streams, and nearby trees provided them with wood for their fires. Around them rolled the long-grass plains, thick with elk and the heavy brown buffalo. The rich central prairie gave them other food—berries, nuts, wild cherries, and the versatile prairie turnip. It was a good time to be alive.

Shadow Fox had no wife. He had been married twice and both wives died. Now he lived with his aunt, his mother's youngest sister, whose own husband had died. She cooked his meals, sewed his clothes, and cared for his lodge. Her name was Pigeon, and she was round and fat.

He gave the baby to her and told her how he had found him in the wolf den.

"He smells bad," said Aunt Pigeon. "He has to have a bath."

She washed him, fed him, and wrapped him inside a warm, skin cradleboard. Now he looked just like any other baby, except that he still growled and tried to bite whenever anyone came near.

In the night Shadow Fox heard wolves howling. He went outside his tipi and stood listening in the dark. They were on the hill above the camp. Shadow Fox knew they were the baby's wolf family. They had come back to the den and found him gone. So they had followed Shadow Fox's trail, and now they were calling to the baby.

He went back into the tipi. The wolves still howled, but the baby slept cozily and didn't hear them at all.

The wolves returned in the morning. The little boy was sitting on the floor, warily watching Shadow Fox and two other men. They had heard about the baby found in the wolf den and came to see this strange thing for themselves.

When the baby heard the wolves, he threw back his head and howled in return. The warriors exchanged glances, shaking their heads in amazement.

"He is not a boy child at all," said one to the other, "but a young wolf in human skin."

The child tried to crawl out of the lodge, but Shadow Fox held him back. At first he bit and growled as before, but then, in rage and frustration, he began to cry. It was the first time he had cried since Shadow Fox found him.

The medicine man smiled as he looked at the red, angry, little face. He laid his hand gently on his head. "Well, little Wolf Brother, so you are human after all."

Once again the other two men looked at one another, with doubt and suspicion in their eyes.

"Do not be too sure," one of them said. "He is certainly no ordinary child. He may not be a child at all but something else . . . a trickster who will bring evil with him."

"We have adopted other children," said Shadow Fox. "Remember High Eagle? No warrior was more brave and loyal then he. And he was born a Crow, who have always been our enemies."

"He was born a human being," said an old man. "Can you say the same for this wolf child?" Shadow Fox did not listen.

The encampment moved every few days in the summer and fall. The wolves followed them from spot to spot, crying and calling. Wolf Brother howled and cried in return.

The villagers stood outside their lodges, listening and talking among themselves.

"The wolves want him back."

"The spirits will be angry if he is not returned."

"It is not natural that a boy child be born to wolves."

"Shadow Fox says he is a human baby who was left with the wolves through some strange accident. He will die if he is taken back to the den."

"Better he should die than bring harm to us."

"Shadow Fox is wise. He would not do anything that is harmful."

"Even a wise man may be blinded by evil spirits."

Black Deer, the chief, spoke. "It is true that this baby is a wonderful child. But why must we think he is evil? Perhaps the spirits have sent him to us as a special mark of favor. Not every band has a child who can speak with the wolves. He may become a great medicine man or warrior who will bring honor to us all. We must not be hasty. Let us wait and see."

The people nodded in agreement. They would wait and see.

TWO

The days grew colder, and the band settled into winter camp. They wouldn't move again until the spring. Game was hard to find, and the wolves spent more time hunting. Soon they didn't come to the village anymore.

Aunt Pigeon worked hard, along with the other women. Most of the work of food gathering was over. The skin tipis were filled with dried meat and dried fruit, herbs and roots, but there was still plenty to do. The women gathered wood, hauled water, tended the fires, and looked after the children.

Aunt Pigeon was an expert needlewoman, whose stiches were finer than anyone's. She made beautiful moccasins, leggings, and shirts, decorating them with fringes and designs of shells, beads, and porcupine quills.

The people told stories all the time. The men gathered together to tell tales of hunting, magic, and battles with other tribes. The women talked as they worked, telling dreams, old legends, singing songs, gossiping about things that went on in the village.

Aunt Pigeon took Wolf Brother with her everywhere. He no longer growled but smiled instead. He was learning a few words in the human tongue. Aunt Pigeon fed him as well as she fed herself, and he was round and fat, too.

The winter passed quickly and spring came again. The snow melted and the new green grass began to grow. Little, fuzzy leaves came out on the trees, and a few small, bright flowers unfolded in the sun.

The villagers had become used to Wolf Brother. By now he

19

was like any other boy and did not seem so strange. He played and ate and slept and spoke baby talk just like any small child. He did not seem unusual in any way. Only now and then a few people muttered that he should not be part of their band.

They moved to a new camp. Wolf Brother was out in front of the tipi, playing in the warm sunshine. Suddenly a wolf howled from the ridge above the camp.

Wolf Brother leaped to his feet, turning his face toward the sound. The wolf called again, and the boy raced through the village as fast as his fat little legs would take him. He had grown a lot over the winter and could run now.

Shadow Fox had been lying in the sun, and now he sprang to his feet and ran after the child. He scooped him up in his arms. Wolf Brother squirmed and yelled to be put down.

Then Shadow Fox thought, the wolves were his family. They kept him alive and warm and fed him when he would have died. Of course they wanted to see each other again.

He carried Wolf Brother through the village and partway up the ridge. He could see the wolves on the crest above him: Wolf Mother, Wolf Father, and Wolf Sister, now quite grown up. He put Wolf Brother down, and the boy began to climb the hill. It was steep for such small legs. He never once looked back but struggled bravely on, gazing at the wolves above him.

They paced back and forth, whining and wagging their tails. Wolf Sister gave a little leap and woofed with excitement. At last she couldn't resist, and she rushed down the hill toward him. The parents followed, and they met on a little flat spot below the crest of the ridge.

They sniffed noses and the wolves wagged their tails some more and Wolf Brother hugged them all. They tried to tell each other everything that had happened during the winter. Wolf Brother gurgled on about how much food he had to eat and how warm he was all the time and how Shadow Fox and Aunt Pigeon were very good to him.

The wolves told him about their hunting trips. They told

him about a big storm in the high mountains when they had lain buried in snow for three days before they could move. Wolf Sister told him how she had almost drowned when she fell through the ice early in the spring and how cold and miserable she had been until she got dry again.

Wolf Brother was too young to understand everything, so he only laughed and gave her a push. She jumped upon him with both front paws and pushed him back. Wolf Brother fell backward, and she leaped on his stomach. He grabbed her around the neck, and they rolled over and over in the grass together, just the way they used to do when they were babies in the den.

Shadow Fox sat below, watching them and smiling. They played hard for a while, and then Wolf Brother became tired. He fell asleep with Wolf Sister on one side of him and Wolf Mother on the the other. Wolf Father lay on top of the ridge, keeping watch.

After a while he got to his feet and walked down to them. He and Wolf Mother sniffed noses. They woke up Wolf Sister, and the three of them turned and looked down the hill at Shadow Fox. Shadow Fox looked quietly back. Then the three wolves turned and trotted up over the hill and out of sight.

Shadow Fox stayed where he was. A little later Wolf Brother felt the empty spaces on both sides of him and he woke up. He began to cry when he saw the wolves were gone.

Shadow Fox stood up. The boy saw the movement and looked down the hill. He stopped crying, wiped his eyes on his hands, and ran down to him. Shadow Fox picked him up and put him on his shoulders. He smiled as he carried him down the hill, for he knew that now the village was Wolf Brother's home.

The wolves came often to visit Wolf Brother during the years that followed. When they came close to the village and called, he went out to play with them. Shadow Fox thought this visiting was a good thing. Perhaps his adopted son would

be a medicine man when he grew up. It would make him special and important to have the wolves as brothers. That would be powerful medicine.

Shadow Fox was a good and wise medicine man. He cured the sick, explained the meaning of dreams and signs, and foretold the future. He had a medicine rattle, decorated with fur and feathers and painted with the designs he had seen on his vision quest when he was a very young man. He must have pleased the Great Spirit, because he was able to help many people. In return, they paid him well.

He didn't often have to hunt to get meat for himself and his family, but he did anyway, just because he liked to hunt. Some of what he didn't use he gave to poor families in the village—those who had no men or whose hunters were old or sick.

Sometimes in the winter, when the snow was on the ground and the wolves were hungry because they could not find food, he gave extra meat to Wolf Brother. Wolf Brother carried it out and gave it to the wolves.

Some people did not like this sharing. They felt that all the food should be kept in the village. Most of the people liked Wolf Brother and had come to agree with Shadow Fox that it was good medicine to have him in their band. He was someone special, brother to the wolves and yet an ordinary boy in other ways.

But some people were still suspicious of him because of his strange beginnings. Perhaps he wasn't human at all. Perhaps someday he would betray them or bring them bad luck. However, most of the band didn't listen to the ones who complained about Wolf Brother.

Wolf Brother and his friend Spotted Pony, both eleven years old, stood in the brush near the creek. A hornets' nest, the same papery color as the dry bark, hung above them on a dead limb. A few hornets buzzed around the entrance and crawled on the sides of the nest.

"Shall we knock it down?" asked Spotted Pony.

"Why not?"

The two boys gathered handfuls of rocks from the creek bed. Cautiously they moved closer to the nest.

"Be ready to run," said Wolf Brother. "Those hornets will be very angry when they come out."

He threw a rock. It missed. He threw another one, and Spotted Pony did too. One of the rocks hit the nest. It wiggled but stayed on the tree. The hornets inside buzzed in warning, and several of them came out, flying in circles beneath the nest.

"We hit it!" they yelled together, and threw some more.

Another rock grazed the side of the nest. The nest wobbled and the buzzing rose in fury. Hornets came swarming out. They swooped back and forth through the bushes, looking for whatever was threatening their home.

The boys kept throwing, laughing and shouting. A stone chunked into the side of the nest with a dull thud. A large piece fell to the ground and suddenly the air was full of hornets, zooming around the boys. The air vibrated with their furious humming.

"Owww!" cried Spotted Pony. "One stung me!" He swatted at his shoulder.

Wolf Brother started to laugh, but all at once a sharp pain stabbed the top of his head. He yelped and brushed at his hair. Another hornet stung his arm.

"Owww! Run! Run! They have found us."

The boys threw away their rocks and stampeded through the brush. The twigs and leaves scratched their skin as they crashed through, but they didn't hurt as much as the hornets.

At last, panting and gasping, they stopped. They both held their breath and listened to see if they could hear the hornets following them. There was only silence.

"My head hurts." Wolf Brother put his hand on the spot.

They heard someone laughing, and two boys stepped out from behind a tree.

24

"Of course you are hurt," said the tall, thin one. "What a silly thing to do! Will you ever outgrow such childish tricks?"

"You are not a man either, Looks-Away," Wolf Brother replied.

"No, but I soon will be. Tomorrow I start preparing for my vision quest."

His voice was boastful. The vision quest was one of the most important events of a warrior's life. When a boy was in his early teens, it was time for him to enter the ranks of the young men. When he felt he was ready, he fasted and purified himself so he would not be displeasing to the spirits. Then he went off alone for several days during which he did not eat or sleep but prayed to the spirits to send him a vision.

If he was fortunate, he would receive a sign to guide him. If he dreamed of an eagle, then perhaps an eagle was to be his spirit helper, who would bring him aid in time of trouble. If he dreamed of herds of buffalo coming to him, perhaps he would be a great hunter.

Each dream had its own meaning. Some dreams were easy to understand. Others were complicated and could be explained only with the help of a medicine man like Shadow Fox, who knew the language of the spirits.

Wolf Brother did not want Looks-Away to know he was impressed that the older boy was so near this important event, so he only shrugged and turned away.

"Come, Spotted Pony," he said. "We need some mud to put on our stings."

Looks-Away and his companion, Owl Feather, followed along as the boys went down to the creek. They mixed water and earth into a paste in the palms of their hands and spread the mud on the hornet stings. It felt cool and soothing.

Looks-Away watched with the one eye that he could control. The other wobbled in its socket. Slowly, like a fish turning in the water, this eye drifted around until it seemed to be looking at a spot across the creek. The eye always refused to focus steadily on one place. It was what had given him his name.

"Children suffer from the stings of insects," Looks-Away said with his scornful smile. "A warrior must face arrows."

"I would not be sorry if you were shot with an arrow," Wolf Brother said.

Looks-Away picked up a handful of mud and threw it at him. Wolf Brother dodged. He was struck on the chest by mud from another direction, thrown by Owl Feather.

Spotted Pony grabbed Owl Feather by the arm. "You stay out of this. Two against one is not fair."

Wolf Brother faced Looks-Away as the taller boy grinned and came toward him with a great handful of mud. He grabbed Wolf Brother's arm, and his long, skinny fingers dug into the flesh. Wolf Brother tried to wrestle out of his grip. He kicked at his shins, but his moccasined feet couldn't hurt the older boy.

Slowly, grinning all the time, Looks-Away rubbed the mud over Wolf Brother's face and head. He smeared it into his mouth and eyes and ground it into his hair. Wolf Brother struggled and flailed helplessly as Looks-Away pulled his arms behind him and turned him to face the other two boys.

"Look at the dirty little boy. He is all muddy. I will help wash him off."

He dragged Wolf Brother out to where the stream was deeper. Over and over again, he plunged his head under the water, until Wolf Brother could hardly draw a breath. He gasped and choked, spitting water, but barely had time to clear his mouth and nose before he was thrust under once more.

He could hear shouting through the roaring in his ears and glimpsed Spotted Pony and Owl Feather splashing toward them through the creek.

"Stop! Stop!" both boys were shouting. "You are going to drown him."

Looks-Away laughed and pushed Wolf Brother away. He fell under the water again. It flooded into his mouth and nose and ached in his throat. He floundered to his feet, gagging and coughing, trying to get air into his lungs.

When he was able to see, Looks-Away and Owl Feather were on the bank. Looks-Away turned toward him, flinging his long, lank hair out of his eyes.

"Little boy," he said, "you are no wolf cub. You are more like a prairie chicken."

He stalked off into the bushes with Owl Feather behind him.

"I have never known anyone as mean as Looks-Away," Spotted Pony said. "Why does he hate you so much?"

Wolf Brother had no answer.

THREE

Wolf Brother sat in front of his lodge. Looks-Away had gone on his vision quest three days ago. The whole village awaited his return. They wanted to know if the spirits would send him a sign and, if they did, what it would be.

Why does Looks-Away hate me so much? Wolf Brother wondered. I have never done anything to him.

Looks-Away seemed to admire Shadow Fox very much. He talked to the medicine man whenever he could and listened carefully to everything he said. He watched what he did and acted as much like him as he could. Shadow Fox was patient with him, as he was with everyone.

Wolf Brother didn't tell Shadow Fox how Looks-Away had nearly drowned him. It was not the first time he had been so rough and cruel, and probably it would not be the last. Wolf Brother always fought back as well as he could and nearly always lost, but he kept his mouth shut and complained to no one.

Sometimes he thought Shadow Fox knew. Sometimes, after Looks-Away left, he would see Shadow Fox looking at him with a certain knowledge in his eyes. He thought perhaps his father was letting him face this trouble himself, as he would have to face things when he became a man.

He sighed and looked around the village. A group of old men sat together, companionably passing a pipe. They were talking about the hunts and battles of days when they were young.

Off to one side, two women worked on an antelope hide. The skin was pegged to the ground with wooden stakes. The fur was down, and the fresh inner side, still red with bits of meat and blood, was turned up. One woman scraped at the meat and fat with a flesher, a blade fastened to an elkhorn handle. The other followed her with a stone scraper. When the hide was completely cleaned, it would be tanned, softened, stretched, and made into clothing.

Two dogs were watching them, hopefully wagging their tails and licking their muzzles. A third dog came trotting over, and one of the others stood up and growled. They faced each other, stiff-legged, their mouths ugly with teeth and gums showing. Suddenly the first one sprang on the newcomer. They tangled together in a ball of legs, teeth, and fur.

Dust from their battle drifted over onto the hide. One of the women gave an exclamation of disgust. Picking up a pegging pole that was lying on the ground, she whacked away at the entangled dogs. They separated and ran yelping off in different directions. The third dog lay down flat on the ground and tried to become invisible. When he saw the woman was ignoring him and he felt safe, he sat up and began wagging his tail again.

There was a shout from outside the village, and all the dogs began to bark. A small group of hunters rode into camp. Wolf Brother recognized them. They were from a neighboring band of Sioux. The two groups often traded and visited back and forth. Looks-Away was riding double behind one of the men.

The horses stopped and he slid off. His knees buckled as he touched the ground and he half fell. He quickly pushed himself upright but wavered unsteadily back and forth. Crooked Leg, Looks-Away's father, and the other men came forward.

"He was unconscious when we found him," one of the men said. "Since he was too weak to walk, we have brought him back to you."

Looks-Away's family took him into their tipi. The visitors dismounted, and the men of the two bands gathered together. They would eat and smoke and talk before the visitors went back to their own village.

Spotted Pony came to sit beside Wolf Brother. "I wonder what he saw," he said.

In a few days people were saying that Looks-Away had received no sign. No message had come to him from the spirits, telling him who or what he should be. He had gone off to seek their word and no word had come. He was still Looks-Away and did not know himself.

Wolf Brother came out of his lodge into the morning light. It was going to be a good day, sunny and cool with a light breeze. He picked up his bow and arrows, saw two other boys, and went over to them.

"It looks like a good day for hunting, Little Eagle. Come try your luck."

Little Eagle turned away. "Go hunt with the wolves."

"You are very cross today." He turned to the other boy. "Blue Shirt, you have a new bow. Will you try it out?"

The boy shook his head. "I will stay with Little Eagle."

Both boys walked away. Wolf Brother heard a step behind him and turned to see Looks-Away and Owl Feather. Owl Feather was younger than Looks-Away. He had passed only twelve winters, but Looks-Away spent most of his time with him. Owl Feather thought he was very important to be the friend of a boy who was nearly ready to join the men.

"What will you do if the boys no longer hunt with you?" Owl Feather asked with a nasty smile.

"Do you not know?" said Looks-Away. "He will go live with the wolves."

"Will you miss him?" asked Owl Feather.

"Not I. I wish he had stayed with the wolves. We do not need him here."

When Wolf Brother did not answer, Looks-Away poked him in the back. "Why do you not return to the wolves? Shadow Fox will be better off without you."

Wolf Brother stopped. "I know you would like to take my place with Shadow Fox. You have wanted this ever since

30

your own father was crippled and no longer able to fight or hunt. But I will not leave. Though the wolves are my friends, I live with the people."

"You are bad medicine," said Looks-Away. He glared angrily at Wolf Brother, but his wandering eye drifted off to gaze beyond his shoulder. "When I was on my vision quest, the spirits warned me against you."

"I thought you were given no signs."

"I was given none about myself, but I was warned against you."

"And what did the spirits say?"

"You and the wolves will harm us. In my vision, I was in my lodge and you were all outside, ripping at the skins with your teeth. You were howling along with the wolf pack. The women and children were crying. There were no men but my father and me. We could not defend the women and children by ourselves. I have always known that you should not be allowed to stay with us."

"I have lived with you nearly all my life, ever since Shadow Fox brought me here," said Wolf Brother. To himself he thought, I would *like* to frighten you, Looks-Away. I would like to bite you with sharp wolf teeth and make you sorry you are so mean to me. But he did not speak out loud. Looks-Away would only try to hurt him again.

"This should not be your home," said Looks-Away. "You came from the wolves. The rest of us were born to people. You alone are different. You do not belong."

"Everyone knows that," said Owl Feather. "It is time for you to go."

Wolf Brother stalked on, and this time they did not follow. Later Spotted Pony came to his lodge.

"Have you heard what Looks-Away is saying?" Wolf Brother asked him.

"Everyone has heard," said Spotted Pony.

"If I went on a vision quest and the spirits did not speak to me about myself, I would keep my mouth shut rather than say bad things about someone else."

"Maybe he thinks any dream is better than none."

Aunt Pigeon had just come back from digging roots, and she heard them talking. "He wants to take the place of Shadow Fox as soon as he is able," she said. "He thinks you will keep him from it. He thinks that if you were not here, he could do so."

"I do not know that I can be a medicine man," said Wolf Brother. "I have had no sign."

"I think Looks-Away made up his sign," said Aunt Pigeon. "And if he continues to lie, the spirits will surely punish him."

She took her knife from its sheath and the turnips from the bag. She began slicing turnips fiercely, scowling as she worked.

Wolf Brother was aware that some of the people looked at him differently now. Looks-Away's story had made them uneasy. Any message from the spirits was important. It was a shame that Looks-Away had come back from his seeking with no word to guide him. But he had come back with a warning, and it might be true. There were omens all around, and bad things would happen if they were ignored.

Wolf Brother was different. Who knew where he came from and what he might really be? They would watch him.

And Wolf Brother knew he was watched. He felt the eyes of people on him whenever he went outside his tipi. They followed him everywhere . . . the eyes of Looks-Away, of Owl Feather, and of Crooked Leg, Looks-Away's father.

He had not always been called Crooked Leg, but he had been hurt during the fall buffalo hunt four years ago. When his pony did not move quickly enough to escape the charge of a wounded buffalo, his leg and hip were crushed. Unfortunately, they had healed badly, and now one leg was twisted and shorter than the other. It was painful for him to ride far. He had been a good hunter and warrior but was no longer able to do much more than hobble around. His family was poor, and Looks-Away was full of bitterness.

"Come, Wolf Brother," Spotted Pony called. "We are going to play Throwing-Them-Off-Their-Horses."

"I do not want to play."

His friend grabbed his arm. "You cannot sit in your lodge all the time. Brown Bear wants you on his side."

"He does?"

"He does not care about the dream of Looks-Away. Come on."

They went to a field outside the village. All the boys were there, sitting bareback on their ponies. They lined up in two rows, one on each side of the field, facing each other. In warm weather they played naked, but now it was too cold. The chill of autumn was on the land.

"Hurry," shouted Brown Bear. "We are waiting for you." Wolf Brother galloped to his side. Brown Bear grinned and slapped his shoulder. Blue Shirt and Little Eagle turned away and would not look at Wolf Brother.

I will not think about them, he said to himself.

He turned his horse, Gisapa, around to face the other team. Spotted Pony was on the other side. He made a face at Wolf Brother and signed that he was going to throw him off his horse. Wolf Brother shook his fist at him.

Some of the older boys and a few men gathered along the edge of the field to watch the game. Wolf Brother saw Looks-Away among them. He seemed to be staring straight at Wolf Brother. Owl Feather was not with him. When Wolf Brother looked back to the field, he was there with the other team. He, too, seemed to be glaring at Wolf Brother.

"I will not let him throw me off," he said to himself.

Brown Bear raised his hand. All the boys swung their ponies to face the other side. He dropped his hand with a yell. With a single great answering whoop, the boys kicked their horses forward. They thundered across the field, shrieking, heels drumming on their horses' ribs to make them go faster.

33

Wolf Brother and Owl Feather galloped straight at each other. Owl Feather was bigger and older, but Wolf Brother would not avoid his challenge. Their horses nearly ran head on into each other, but they swerved just enough at the last moment to avoid a collision. Owl Feather's leg smashed into Wolf Brother. His knee felt as though it were broken, but he clamped his legs tighter around Gisapa's sides and held on. Owl Feather grabbed his arm and hauled on it. Wolf Brother pulled against him, but Owl Feather was stronger and he could feel himself being dragged off. If he fell to the ground he was "dead" and out of the game.

He kicked Gisapa forward and lunged all his weight against Owl Feather at the same time. The trick almost worked. Owl Feather tipped backward as the horses crashed into each other, but he caught his balance in time. Owl Feather's mount reared and his head broke their hold.

They whirled their plunging horses to face each other. Owl Feather looked grim, as though it were not a game they played but a contest for blood. Wolf Brother knew he could not let the older boy get hold of him again. He didn't have the size or strength to stand against him long.

Before he was ready, Owl Feather shouted deep in his throat and came plunging at him. Wolf Brother flung up his right hand as though he were going to grab for Owl Feather's head. At the last minute, he ducked low on Gisapa's neck and bobbed up behind Owl Feather's arm. Reaching back, he made a wild grab at Owl Feather and his hand hooked under his chin. Flailing at the air, Owl Feather flipped backward over his horse's rump and fell to the ground.

Wolf Brother yelled in triumph. It had been partly luck that his desparate backward clutch had found a mark, but luck was part of any battle. He glanced toward the spectators and saw Looks-Away turn aside as though he had not been watching.

Wolf Brother grinned and returned to the game. Sweating horses raced back and forth across the field. They dodged and

spun and plunged into each other, grunting and snorting. The boys whooped and grunted and sweated too. Their black heads glistened like the wings of ravens in the sun.

There were several boys on the ground, scrambling out of the way of the charging horses, some of them riderless, that milled across the field. A small boy, carried away by the excitement and yelling ferociously, hurled himself at Wolf Brother. Wolf Brother easily dumped him on the ground.

Then he saw Spotted Pony charging toward him, grinning. He kicked Gisapa forward, and they plunged together. Their arms and hands tangled, their bodies straining back and forth, while their legs clamped like iron around their horses. Spotted Pony's grin turned into a bared-teeth snarl of determination. He and Wolf Brother surged back and forth, not trying any tricks, just grimly pitting each one's strength against the other.

Slowly, slowly, Wolf Brother slipped off his horse. It was too late to try a trick, and he was too tired anyway. He slid to the ground, and Spotted Pony counted coup on his head. Then he turned with a shout and hurled his hard, square body at another victim.

Wolf Brother shook his head. Spotted Pony could always beat him at Throwing-Them-Off-Their-Horses, but then he could beat almost everyone else. He was strong as a bear and could rarely be dislodged from his horse.

Wolf Brother rubbed his aching arms and walked to the side of the field with Gisapa trailing behind.

"You did well, Wolf Brother, to throw off Owl Feather, who is older," said one of the old men, Many Buffalo, in his high, thin voice.

Wolf Brother nodded, feeling proud. Two other men walked away, murmuring to each other. Once they would have complimented him too, but now they remembered Looks-Away's dream and they did not speak.

FOUR

It was a strange winter for Wolf Brother. For the first time he realized he was different from the other people. He had always known that he was born outside the band, but it had never seemed important before. Most of his eleven years—his whole lifetime—had been lived with this band.

But eleven years wasn't very long to some of the older people. They wondered who his real parents had been and why the wolves had cared for him. Now Wolf Brother wondered about these things too.

He was a member of this band only by adoption. First he had belonged to the wolves, and now he went back to them whenever he chose. He hunted and slept with them in the summers, took food to them in the winters.

His wolf parents had a new litter of puppies every year, and they were his brothers and sisters. Wolf Sister had grown up and had a mate of her own, named Blackfoot. She had puppies, and Wolf Brother was an uncle to them. Sometimes he baby-sat for her while she went off to hunt or rest. He lay on the ground and let the puppies jump and chew on him, as he had once played with Wolf Father. By now he was related to nearly every wolf for miles around.

He didn't have to stay with the people. He had another family, another way of life waiting for him. And the wolves were never critical. They accepted him just as he was and let him come and go as he wanted. If Looks-Away or anyone else made the human part of his life too hard, he had some other place to go. It was a comforting thought.

Looks-Away's vision came again. Or so he said. Even Shadow Fox shook his head when he heard it had come for the second time. Those people who had spoken against Wolf Brother from

the beginning were glad to hear of the dreams. They felt they had been right all along, and there was something dangerous about bringing this mysterious child into their band.

The winter was short and dry, with very little rain or snow. The wind blew, howling across the wide, sweeping prairie, whining around the lodges huddled in the shelter of rocks and valleys. The sky stayed empty. The clouds were blown away before they could form, and the earth stayed brown and bare.

Spring came too early. Instead of being happy, the old people frowned. It was unnatural and out of its place and time. "Water will be scarce this year," they said. Anxiously they watched the omens, and all of them were bad.

Wolf Brother and Spotted Pony practiced with their bows and arrows. They took turns shooting at a target near Wolf Brother's tipi.

Spotted Pony aimed and let his arrow fly. It missed the target. It was Wolf Brother's turn to shoot, and he hit near the center of the mark.

Spotted Pony scuffed his feet. "I could shoot better if I were not so hungry," he said. "I am so empty my arm is weak."

"Come inside," Wolf Brother said. "Aunt Pigeon will feed us."

They went into the lodge and dipped out of the pot that was simmering over the fire. Something was always cooking there, some kind of meat stew flavored with roots, herbs, and leaves. Sometimes whole chunks of meat were roasted. The people had no special mealtimes but ate whenever they were hungry. As the food in the pot was eaten, Aunt Pigeon added more, keeping it full. The tipi was always rich with the smell of woodsmoke and good food.

"Are you back again?" she grumbled. "You boys have no bottom to your stomachs."

She sounded cross, but they both knew she really didn't mind. She just liked to complain.

Shadow Fox sat on the floor, leaning on a backrest made of

willow sticks. He was smoking his pipe and meditating. Smoking was an important part of his life. The smoke that drifted toward the sky carried his prayers with it to the spirit world. The boys ate quietly so they would not disturb him.

The camp dogs barked and then became still as they recognized who was coming. Hoofbeats sounded on the ground outside and stopped in front of Shadow Fox's lodge. A warrior named Quick Hand entered through the flap and stood on the right side of the lodge. Shadow Fox put down his pipe and signed for him to sit beside him.

"There are strangers in our valley," said Quick Hand.

"Who are they?"

"I think they are Assiniboin."

"They do not usually come this far south."

"No, they do not," agreed Quick Hand.

"Where did you see them?"

"Their camp is in the cottonwoods by the little creek. I saw the smoke from their cooking fires as I came back from hunting. I went close to their camp and climbed one of the trees to see better. They have a few women and children with them."

"Have you told Black Deer?"

Quick Hand shook his head. "Black Deer is an old man. He does not move much anymore."

"Black Deer is the chief. He must be told. I will go with you."

The two men left the tipi, and Wolf Brother and Spotted Pony trailed along behind. Black Deer was sitting in front of his lodge, old and humped in his fringed shirt. He had been chief for as long as most of the young men could remember. Smoking his pipe, he listened to Quick Hand's story.

"We will wait awhile," he said, after a long pause in which he puffed out several mouthfuls of smoke. "We have been at peace for a long time. Neither the Cheyenne nor the Crow have sent war parties against us for many moons. If these people do not bother us, we will not bother them."

"Perhaps we should sent a small scouting party, just to see

who they are and what they want," Shadow Fox said.

"We will wait," Black Deer replied, and smoked his pipe.

One of the young men whispered to another. "His rheumatism bothers him. That is why he does not want to ride."

"He is still chief," said the other.

Shadow Fox returned to his lodge. His face was grave, and Wolf Brother knew he was concerned. It would show disrespect to Black Deer if anyone went to the other camp now. Just the same during the next two days hunters several times chanced to pass the camp on the little creek. Quietly they climbed the cottonwood trees and looked at the few scraggly tipis. The people seemed poor and harmless, hardly leaving their lodges. The boys would have gone too, but they were forbidden. They must stay close to their village while there were strangers in the valley.

Shadow Fox searched the sky and the wind. He watched the flight of birds and the actions of animals. He was looking for omens but found none.

Wolf Brother wakened abruptly. The dark tent shook with sound. The earth trembled beneath him, and the air rang with screams and cries.

At first he could not understand what was happening, and he was filled with blind terror. He lay stiffly in his robes, staring straight up, and the beating of his heart shook his whole body. Then he knew the drumming sounds that rocked the earth were horses' hoofbeats. The yells and shouts were the cries of frightened women and children.

Wolf Brother jumped to his feet and fumbled on the floor for his little bow and arrows. It was early dawn, and now that he was really awake he could see that Shadow Fox's place was empty. The medicine man was already outside. He scrambled to the door, but before he could duck through, Aunt Pigeon grabbed him from behind.

"No, Wolf Brother," she cried. "You are still too young to fight. Stay here."

He tried to wrestle free. "I am not too young. Let me go!"

"Your father told me to make you stay. You must obey him."

He did have to obey Shadow Fox, even if he didn't want to. He let Aunt Pigeon lead him away from the opening, but he still kept hold of his bow and arrows. They sat in the middle of the lodge, and he held the weapon on his knees, pointed at the door. Together they listened to the battle sounds around them.

They didn't last very long. Soon the yelling died away and the thunder of the horses faded in the distance. Wolf Brother went outside, and Aunt Pigeon followed.

Warriors ran back and forth in the cold dawn light, shouting to each other and to their families. Women and children huddled together in the openings of tipis. A group of men were gathered in the middle of the village, and Wolf Brother went over to them. Shadow Fox was there, kneeling on the ground. Black Deer, the old chief, lay before him. There was an arrow in his shoulder, and two braves held him down while the medicine man cut it out.

Another man lay to one side, but he did not move at all. Already the women were wailing above him, and soon they would gash themselves with knives, hack off their hair, and rub themselves with ashes in grief for the dead.

"What happened?" Wolf Brother asked one of the young men.

"It was the strangers. They have stolen some of our horses and killed one of our men. We should have driven them away before they did this to us."

The men carried Black Deer to his lodge, and Wolf Brother followed. Torches burned inside as they laid him on his skins. The old man's face looked like a skull's, sharp and bony in the flaring light. His eyes were dark and hooded, sunk far back into shadows. Sweat ran down his face, and blood and sweat together soaked his deerskin shirt.

"I am chief no longer," he said in a hard, strong voice that sounded as though he forced it out between clenched teeth.

"I let the raiders surprise us. I am too old and my bones hurt too much. My son, Buffalo Calf, is a war chief. Listen to his words."

He sank back and closed his eyes. His wife and daughters gathered around him as the men went outside. Buffalo Calf picked up his lance and held it in the air.

"I will seek out our enemies," he cried. "Who will ride with me?"

The warriors all shouted and saluted with their weapons. Wolf Brother stood to one side as they rushed around, gathering food, weapons, and rounding up the horses that were left.

Shadow Fox came and put his hand on his shoulder. "Wolf Brother, you must be the man in our lodge while I am gone."

"I want to come along," he said, but he spoke without hope. He knew he could not go.

"Aunt Pigeon needs you here. Take care until I return."

He sprang upon his horse, and the animal half reared as he whirled around. Other horses and riders surged back and forth, rocketing through the spaces between the tipis. Dogs ran in and out, barking and yelping and dodging the flying hooves. Men shouted and pounded on their leather shields. Buffalo Calf rode out on his big, red horse. With a wild yell he kicked him into a run. All the horses and warriors swept out of the village and vanished into the dawn.

A shower of sparks bloomed in the fire and then died down. A chill wind swirled through the camp, shaking the flaps on the lodges. The women wept and wailed as they prepared the dead brave for burial.

Wolf Brother looked toward the light growing in the east. It was cold and far away and brought no comfort. He went inside and wrapped himself in his robes, but sleep did not come.

FIVE

Days passed and the men did not return. Because it was so early in the spring, the lodges were nearly empty of food. The winter stores were almost used up and had not been replaced. Wolf Brother, Spotted Pony, and the other boys, as well as the old men, went out to hunt every day. Sometimes they came back with rabbits, squirrels, or birds, but there were many people in the village and the small game was not enough to feed them all. The women fished and dug what early roots they could find.

Wolf Brother noticed that Aunt Pigeon was eating less than usual. "Are you sick, Auntie?" he asked.

"No," she said. "I am too fat. If I eat less, I will be thinner."

He knew she had never before thought she was too fat. In fact, she had been proud of her size and sometimes bragged to the other women in the village, saying, "Shadow Fox is such a good man. Look how well he feeds his old aunt. I eat as much as I can, and there is always more."

Wolf Brother knew she was eating less because they were running low on food. He hunted all the next day but came back without a single thing. That night he just nibbled a little at what was in the pot.

"Eat more," said Aunt Pigeon. "You are a growing boy and need more than that."

"I am not hungry."

Aunt Pigeon sighed and reached into the pot. She picked out a large piece of meat and pushed it between his lips. "One more bite, Wolf Brother. You have to keep strong enough to

hunt. I will fish again tomorrow, and maybe I will catch something this time. And the men will soon be home."

The village was no longer noisy. The children played quiet
games, and the little ones were cross and cried a lot over
nothing. The village dogs were never fat, and now they were
thinner than ever. No one gave them scraps anymore and
several of them went away, perhaps to look for food on their
own. Only the horses were the same. They had all the grass
they could eat.

Aunt Pigeon no longer sang and chattered while she sewed.
She walked a little bent over, and Wolf Brother knew her
stomach hurt from hunger. His hurt too sometimes, although
he tried to pretend it did not. Several times a day someone
climbed the hill above the village to see if the warriors were
returning, but they always came down without seeing anything.

Late one afternoon the chorus of the dogs told that someone
was approaching. Wolf Brother and Aunt Pigeon hurried with
the others to see who it would be.

It was Looks-Away coming slowly, alone and on foot. This
was the first time he had gone with the men on a war party,
and now he was back before anyone else. He looked tired and
dirty and bedraggled.

"Where are the men?" asked Crooked Leg.

"They are still chasing the horse thieves. My own horse
fell and broke his leg. It would have slowed the others down
if one horse had to carry two riders. I came back so they could
go faster."

Looks-Away went to his lodge with his father, his mother,
and his three little sisters around him. His feet must have hurt
because he limped nearly as much as Crooked Leg. Wolf
Brother could not tell if he looked at him or not, because one
eye went one way and one the other.

Spotted Pony and Wolf Brother hunted together every day.
Every day Spotted Pony seemed a little quieter and more
troubled.

45

"You must be very hungry," Wolf Brother said at last. "Come to my lodge tonight. We still have enough to feed you."

"No, we still have food. But I do not like what Looks-Away and his family are saying about you. More and more people are listening to them all the time."

"What are they saying?" asked Wolf Brother.

"They say it is your fault we are hungry. If you had not given so much meat to the wolves last winter, we would have more dried meat now. And Looks-Away will not let them forget what he dreamed. That dream is more important than ever."

A hollow ache, deeper than any physical pain, filled Wolf Brother. He felt love and loyalty to both the wolves and the people. Always he had felt himself fortunate to belong to two families, and one was as important as the other. Now he was being pushed to the point where he might have to choose between them. It would not be easy.

The people in a village formed a special unit. Each member of the band was truly brother and sister to all members. They depended upon each other for everything—for food, shelter, companionship, care in sickness and old age.

People rarely left their own band unless they married into another. They did not move from group to group, making new friends as they went. They stayed where they belonged, where their parents and grandparents and great-grandparents had always been. Everyone knew who everyone else was and knew their histories and all their family's histories.

Really important events, which affected the whole band, were recorded on skin charts called "winter counts." A picture was drawn of the most important event of each year. It might be an eclipse, the death of a chief, a victory over another tribe. Each year had its own symbol.

Other happenings—exceptional acts of bravery, displays of power or magic, great hunts and battles—were made into songs and stories. Some warriors who had died before even the oldest grandmother was born still lived on in memory as the story of their deeds was told over and over again. The songs and legends were like threads, thin but strong, connecting each person to other members of the band. Old tales spun around the people like spider webs, linking them to the past.

Only Wolf Brother could claim no inheritance from the songs and stories. He was a stray cub found in a wolf den, neither animal nor human, but something in between.

Another day passed, and he asked Spotted Pony, "What are they saying about me now?"

Spotted Pony did not answer.

"Tell me," said Wolf Brother. "I must know."

"It is not everyone. But some say we should drive you from the village. If you care so much about the wolves, they think you should live with them all the time. They say you have brought us these bad times."

I wonder if they are right, Wolf Brother thought. Perhaps I was meant to stay with the wolves and Shadow Fox was wrong to bring me here. If the spirits put me with the wolves, they may be angry that I left them.

Maybe I should go back. It would be easy to leave some of the people, but how could I leave Spotted Pony and Shadow Fox and Aunt Pigeon? They do not want me to go, and I would miss them, even though I could come back and visit.

Why do I have this choice to make? Why was I not born in the village, like Spotted Pony and everyone else? Why could I not know, without doubt, where I am supposed to be? I am the only one in the village who does not know his real home.

When the boys got back to camp, they heard the sound of wailing. Wolf Brother ran to his lodge.

"What has happened?" he cried to Aunt Pigeon.

"It is Red Bird's old grandmother. They thought she was eating, but instead she was saving the food. She hid it under her blanket, and they found it after she died. I am going over

48

there now. You stay in the lodge until I come back. Some of the foolish people are saying you are to blame."

"I know," said Wolf Brother in a small voice.

Aunt Pigeon hugged him. "It is not your fault, and most of them know it. But there are always some who like to blame others when things go wrong."

Wolf Brother looked in the pot after she left. There was a thin, watery soup, mostly roots and dried leaves, instead of the thick meat stew that usually bubbled there. When he was out hunting, he had been very hungry. The pain he felt in his stomach now did not come from emptiness, however, and he could not eat.

He sat cross-legged on his robe. If only Shadow Fox and the other hunters would come, maybe everything would be all right again.

But another slow day passed, and the men did not return. He and Spotted Pony hunted again and came home empty-handed.

Looks-Away, Little Eagle, Blue Shirt, and some other boys were talking among themselves in the village. They didn't say anything as the two boys walked by, but their eyes struck Wolf Brother as hard as stones.

"Wolf Brother, go back to the wolves," hissed Looks-Away after they passed.

"Go back to the wolves," repeated a small boy.

Several little ones followed behind him as he went to his lodge. "Go to the wolves," they chanted. "Go to the wolves. Then we will eat again."

Wolf Brother wanted to run, but he walked steadily without hurrying. Several adults watched, but no one stopped the boys from tormenting him. As he lifted the flap on his lodge, he turned to Spotted Pony. They looked at each other without words. The hostility was as hard for Spotted Pony as it was for him, and neither one of them could help the other.

He stepped inside the shadowy safety of his lodge and closed the flap. The boys ran around outside for a few more minutes, still chanting, and then they went away.

In the gray light of early morning, Wolf Brother was awakened by the sound of cries and moanings. He sat up and looked at Aunt Pigeon. There were big shadows under her eyes, and her once-plump cheeks looked sunken.

"I will see who has died," she said, and went out of the tent. She put her head in a few minutes later. "It is the new baby born to Yellow Robe. The baby was weak at birth and probably would not have lived anyway. Go back to sleep if you can. I must help the women."

But Wolf Brother did not go back to sleep. He put on his moccasins as soon as she was gone. The fire had gone out in the night, but he ate a little of the cold soup. He knew what he must do.

Everything was quiet except for the keening of the women at the other end of the village. Two thin dogs raised their heads as he passed by, but neither barked. The sun was not up, but a crack of golden light split the sky from the eastern mountains. He took Gisapa and rode off into the hills.

SIX

Wolf Brother rode out to a high hill. He tied Gisapa to a tree at the base and climbed up on foot. It was bare on top except for several big rocks and boulders.

The sun was up when he got to the summit, bursting over the hills in a flood of yellow light. Long purple shadows still lay in the valleys, but the upper parts of the earth were drenched in warmth and color. A dawn wind moved around him, clean and cold.

Wolf Brother knew other things moved too, the spirits of the air and the mountains. He could feel them shifting and sighing, and he knew they were as clean and as cold as the wind. He said a prayer to get their attention, to let them know that he was there and that he and the village people needed their help.

The wind stopped. Perhaps the spirits stopped too. All the morning world was without sound.

Wolf Brother tipped back his head, stretched his throat, and howled. When he had been a baby and howled, the sound had been a tiny, gurgling one, a funny imitation of a wolf. Now it was a real wolf cry, long, strong, and spine-tingling. It sailed out from the mountain top and filled all the silent morning. It drifted over the grasses and through the trees and wound down canyons and spread like dust over the land.

Two more times he howled, and then he sat down with his back against the biggest rock to wait. The wolves heard him calling. They picked up his message and passed it on, relaying it to others farther away. It was a special, urgent message, telling them all to come, telling them Wolf Brother needed them.

And one by one, they came. Wolf Father and Wolf Mother came first, and then Wolf Sister and Blackfoot. They touched noses and the wolves wagged their tails. They lay down, panting a little, to wait for the others. All morning they gathered, the gray, shadowy shapes filling the top of the hill. They came padding on big leathery paws, their metallic eyes glittering in the sun.

Wolf Brother greeted each one. When they were all there, he climbed up on a rock and spoke to them. He told them how the strangers had raided his village, although the wolves knew that already. They nearly always knew what was happening in their country. He told them that all the hunters were away chasing the raiders and that food in the village was almost gone. He told them that the people were starting to die from hunger. He reminded them of the many times when he and his adopted father had fed them. Now he needed their help.

One by one the wolves came up to him and touched noses. They told him not to worry, they would do what they could, and then they went away. When the last one was gone, Wolf Brother said another little prayer, this time thanking the spirits for hearing his words.

He got his horse and returned to the village. When he rode in, he could see that everyone was worried. They stood in little groups, talking in low tones, and turned to look sullenly at him as he came up.

"It is going to be all right," he called to the first group. "I talked to the wolves, and they will bring us food."

He could see they didn't believe him.

"It is true," he shouted. "We helped the wolves, by feeding them before, and they will feed us now."

No one spoke. They only looked at him with hard dark eyes.

"I just came back from the council hill. They all came when I called them. They will help us."

"Go get Aunt Pigeon," one of the old women said. "Hunger has made him crazy. Wolves never help anyone."

"I am not crazy. Remember, the wolves are my brothers."

"Then go live with them," Looks-Away said. "You bring us nothing but misfortune."

"You are as much wolf as human," said Crooked Leg. "Bad things keep happening since you came." His hand rubbed up and down the thigh of his lame leg.

Wolf Brother saw Spotted Pony come out of his lodge, and he ran over to him. "Spotted Pony, I talked to the wolves, and they will bring us food. Surely you believe me?"

Spotted Pony looked at him a minute. "Yes, I do. If you say it, it is true."

Looks-Away laughed harshly. The others shook their heads and turned away. Aunt Pigeon came puffing. "What is this? What are you saying?"

"I went out to talk to the wolves. They will bring us food. Aunt Pigeon, you must believe me."

She looked at him sadly. "I wish Shadow Fox would come home. Why are they staying away so long? They must know we are hungry. Come inside, little one. There is still some soup."

That night everyone in the village gathered together, except Wolf Brother, who stayed in his lodge. Aunt Pigeon went out for a while and when she came back, she looked sadder than before.

"They are talking about me," he said.

"Yes, they are. Hunger is making everyone mean and miserable. More of them are saying that you should leave the village. But do not worry. You still have many friends."

"Tomorrow everything will be all right," said Wolf Brother.

Aunt Pigeon sighed and covered her head with her robe.

Early the next afternoon, Wolf Father howled from the ridge. Wolf Brother ran out of his tipi.

"They have come," he shouted. "The wolves have come."

He ran through the village, yelling, "Follow me. Now we will have food."

People came out of their lodges and looked at him, some sadly, some with cold, hostile faces. Looks-Away was smiling a one-sided smile of triumph. "Little Wolf Brother, you have lost your mind. No one will go with you."

Spotted Pony came up. "I will go with you."

The two boys ran out of the village and climbed the hill. Wolf Father and three others were sitting in a row on the top. Their long red tongues hung out. They looked tired and proud and happy. In front of them was a pile of game: rabbits, birds, mice, and squirrels.

Wolf Brother shouted with joy. He hugged the wolves, and they licked his face. Then they went away. He and Spotted Pony picked up an animal in each hand and raced down the hill to the village. A little girl was the first to see the game.

"Look!" she cried. "He has a rabbit. And a bird, too."

"There is more on the hill. Go and see," cried Wolf Brother.

Puffing, Aunt Pigeon climbed up, with Many Buffalo and some of the others following. Wolf Brother put the game inside his lodge and ran back.

Many Buffalo had reached the pile of rabbits and squirrels. He picked one up and held it high above his head. "Wolf Brother is right. The wolves have brought us food," he shouted.

Then other people went up the hill. Some ran eagerly, calling thanks to Wolf Brother as they went. But some went slowly, grudgingly, their faces set in scowls, their feet scuffing the ground. Only hunger compelled them. If they had not been so hungry, they would not have gone.

Looks-Away, Owl Feather, and Crooked Leg did not go. They went into their lodges and closed the flaps. One of Looks-Away's little sisters ran up and grabbed two squirrels. She took one to her lodge and one to Owl Feather's family, but the men did not come out.

"I do not understand," Wolf Brother said to Aunt Pigeon. "I

thought they would be pleased. The wolves helped us as I said they would. Why are they not pleased?"

"Some people would rather be right than eat," Aunt Pigeon said sourly. "It is hard to admit you have been wrong. But we will not think about that tonight. We will think about the delicious rabbit stew instead. Come along, Wolf Brother. I am very pleased with you."

Wolf Brother went with her, but all his happiness had curdled to lumps inside him. He knew how hard the wolves had worked to gather the food. Many of them would go hungry tonight so the villagers could eat. The wolves did not care about the villagers, but they did care about him, and what greater proof than that they would bring their own food and give it to him.

Wolves are better than people, he thought.

But then he remembered that Shadow Fox was the one who had first shared meat from his hunt with the wolves. Many Buffalo and Old Chief Black Deer and his son, Buffalo Calf, had given food too. They had always felt Wolf Brother's kinship with the wolves was good medicine. They felt that feeding the wolves was pleasing to the spirits, and so, in turn, the spirits would look kindly upon them when they needed help.

Aunt Pigeon joked and sang as she cooked the rabbit, and finally Wolf Brother smiled too. She was trying hard to make him feel good. He would be ungrateful not to respond.

"If it were not for you and Shadow Fox and Spotted Pony, I would leave tonight and go with the wolves forever," he said.

"I am not surprised to hear you say so," she replied. "I knew you must be thinking about it. But if you ever decide you must go, talk to Shadow Fox first."

"I will."

"Now," said Aunt Pigeon, "we can eat."

The men came back two days later. They arrived late in the day, tired, dusty, and almost as bedraggled as Looks-Away had been. They did not bring the stolen horses with them, and they had not caught the raiders. However, they had hunted on the way home, so the village had food once more.

Things seemed normal again, but Wolf Brother knew they were not. The boys were reluctant to include him in their games and contests. They let him play if he joined them, but they didn't ask him anymore. Only Spotted Pony and Brown Bear were his friends, and Brown Bear was moody. His mother did not want him to play with Wolf Brother, and he was angry and confused.

Shadow Fox listened when Wolf Brother told him all that had happened while he was gone. "No matter what you do, you cannot make everyone happy. All you can do is what seems best, and most people will understand. You will have to forget the rest of them."

He puffed on his pipe. "What did you think when Looks-Away came back alone?"

"He said his horse broke his leg and that riding double would slow you down. He came back so you could go faster."

"It was his own foolishness that caused his horse to fall. He could not keep up with the rest of us. He tried to use a shortcut to catch up and jumped his horse over a ravine. It was too far, and he killed his horse.

"There are many things Looks-Away cannot do well. He does not understand horses. He is not strong. He cannot shoot well with a bow and arrow, because he cannot see well. He will never be a great hunter or warrior. Have you ever thought it strange that he spends his time with Owl Feather and boys who are much younger? Looks-Away is old enough to take his place among the men, and yet he lingers with the boys. He cannot keep up with young men his own age."

Amazement flooded Wolf Brother. He had never thought of Looks-Away in this manner. He was bigger and older, so he had never noticed the things he lacked. But it was true that Looks-Away, though tall, was thin as a stick and that he was awkward and ill at ease with those of his own age.

"Looks-Away must be able to take care of his family, since his father is no longer able," Shadow Fox went on. "He has no brothers, and there are three little sisters and his mother to look after. Like anyone else, Looks-Away wants respect and a place in the band. If he cannot find it as a hunter and warrior, he hopes to find it as a medicine man. He thinks you stand in his way."

"I do not know that I can be a medicine man," said Wolf Brother.

"I do not know either," said Shadow Fox. "I do not think a man chooses to be one. I think the spirits choose the man. Looks-Away may not know this yet."

"Do you think it would help if I talked to Looks-Away and told him I do not want to get in his way?"

Shadow Fox shook his head. "No. Looks-Away has many difficulties, and he blames them all on you. He would not hear anything you said."

"Then what can I do?"

"We will have to wait," said Shadow Fox.

Wait! It was so unfair! Everyone was always blaming him for everything that went wrong.

"I do not want to wait," Wolf Brother said angrily. "What more do they want? I fed the whole tribe when they were hungry, even Looks-Away, who has never been anything but mean to me. Why is he not grateful? I could have had the wolves bring food just for myself and Aunt Pigeon and Spotted Pony and let everyone else starve to death. That is what I should have done . . . let them all starve."

"You have a reason to be angry," said Shadow Fox.

"If things do not get better soon, I will not stay here. I do not have to live here. I can go back to the wolves."

"That is true," said Shadow Fox. "But it is a very serious decision. You must think it over carefully before you decide if you want to live as a wolf or as a human being. You will be deciding where you belong."

SEVEN

It was the hottest part of the summer. All during the day the sun filled the whole sky. The sky itself seemed shiny, almost silver-colored, and it hurt the eyes to look at it.

The water was the only place to be cool. Wolf Brother and Spotted Pony were swimming in the creek near the village. They floated quietly on their backs, looking up into the leaves of the trees above them. The rest of the boys from the village laughed and splashed noisily at the other end of the pool. Brown Bear was with them.

Suddenly they heard voices calling, and they stood up to see two girls running along the shore toward them.

"Wolf Brother. Wolf Brother," one of them cried.

Wolf Brother didn't like this girl very much. She was older than he was, quite silly, and always making a big fuss over nothing.

"Yes, Little Squirrel. I hear you."

She and her cousin stopped by the water's edge. They looked as if they had run a long way, and their faces were wet with sweat. One of Little Squirrel's braids was coming out, and twigs were tangled in her hair. The other girl was carrying an empty basket in her hand. They were both panting and gasping for breath.

"Wolf Brother," Little Squirrel wheezed, "your wolves are trying to kill us."

Wolf Brother looked at Spotted Pony, who rolled his eyes and made a face.

"Wolves will not hurt you," said Wolf Brother.

59

"These tried. They ran out of the bushes and chased us, growling and howling all the time."

"That is true," said the other girl, named Pretty Bird. "They really did."

"I cannot believe you," said Wolf Brother. "None of the wolves would harm a person, especially one from this village."

"This one tried. We were lucky to escape with our lives."

"First you say 'they,' and now you say 'one,'" said Spotted Pony. "How many were there?"

"A whole pack," said Little Squirrel.

"One," said Pretty Bird.

"How many?" asked Wolf Brother.

Both girls began to talk at the same time, yelling and interrupting each other.

Wolf Brother spat into the water in disgust. "I cannot understand either of you. I think you have sunstroke."

He dove underwater and swam to the other side of the creek. Spotted Pony followed him. When they came up, they saw the girls running to the village.

"I suppose we had better go in," said Wolf Brother. "Their story is sure to make things worse than they are already."

It was not a good summer. Since the winter had been so dry, creeks and springs that normally ran full were low or entirely empty. Game was scarce and hard to find. The fruit and berries were small, hard, and sour. A sickness ran through the village, and weeks later many were still weak and listless. It seemed that all good things were withheld and only misfortune came. The villagers made offerings, prayers, and sacrifices, but the spirits had turned their faces from them and would not listen.

In times such as these, even the people who were still friendly to Wolf Brother would be apt to believe things against him.

When they got to the village, Little Squirrel and Pretty Bird were surrounded by a small group of people. They were still shouting and interrupting each other, trying to tell their story at the same time.

"We were berry picking—"

"We heard this awful howling—"

"A whole pack of wolves—"

"It chased us a mile—"

"They tried to kill us—"

"We were almost eaten alive!"

Their grandfather, Many Buffalo, raised his hands. "Hush!" he roared.

Little Squirrel and Pretty Bird both stopped talking.

"Where are the berries your mothers sent you to pick?"

"We lost them running from the wolves."

"I lost my basket, too."

"I think you are lazy girls who did not want to pick berries in the hot sun. You are making up this story to excuse yourselves."

"No, no. It really happened. We heard growling and the wolf came running after us—"

"Enough!" Many Buffalo roared again. "Everyone knows that the wolves would never harm anyone from this village. They are Wolf Brother's kin. Remember how they fed us four moons ago? Now hush your foolish tongues. Tomorrow you will go out berry picking, and you will come back with your baskets full. You will not tell us any more wild stories to hide your laziness."

The girls walked quietly away with their heads down. As Pretty Bird passed him, Wolf Brother saw tears in her eyes.

Later in the day, Wolf Brother watched as Aunt Pigeon sat in front of the lodge making pemmican. The dried buffalo meat had all the sinew and gristle removed so it would be tender. She pounded it on a dish-shaped rock, mixing in berries as she worked, and packed the mixture in a parfleche bag. This bag was made of cured hide that had all the hair scraped off and was dried on a frame. When the bag was full of meat and berries, she poured melted fat over it and tied it tightly shut for storage.

Wolf Brother's mouth watered as he watched. Of all the dried foods, pemmican was the best. He would rather eat it than almost anything.

Shadow Fox came and crouched down to dip into the cooking pot.

"Little Squirrel and Pretty Bird told a wild story today," Wolf Brother said to him.

"I heard it."

"Many Buffalo said they were lying. He said they were too lazy to pick berries in the hot sun and made up an excuse."

"It could be so," said Shadow Fox. "Little Squirrel is often silly."

"Pretty Bird is not so bad. She had tears in her eyes when her grandfather accused her."

"Do you think a pack of wolves did chase them?" asked his father.

"No, such a thing would never happen. And yet. . . ."

Shadow Fox ate a little more. "You are learning, my son. Never believe everything anyone tells you. And yet never forget that anything is possible. If you can walk a narrow line between believing everything and nothing, you will be a wise man."

The next morning Wolf Brother went to Pretty Bird's lodge. He called and she came out, looking crossly at him.

"What do you want?"

"I want you to show me where you were when the wolves chased you."

"You said you did not believe us."

"It is hard to believe you, but I would like to see the place."

"I have to pick berries today."

"Bring your basket and we will go."

"I do not want to go back to where we saw the wolf."

"So it was only one? But it does not matter. There will be no wolf this morning. Besides, I will be with you, and you know the wolves and I are one family."

"Little Squirrel has to come too."

He scowled. He would rather go without her, but he knew she had to obey her grandfather.

Little Squirrel did not want to go. She stood sulkily by her lodge when Pretty Bird called her outside and looked out of the corners of her eyes at Wolf Brother.

"Looks-Away's sister told me you and the wolves are going to destroy the village."

Pretty Bird answered before Wolf Brother could reply. "Grandfather told you not to listen. Looks-Away is jealous of Wolf Brother. Are you going to believe him or your own grandfather?"

"I cannot forget Looks-Away's dream. Dreams are important, especially one from a vision quest."

Wolf Brother was too tired of the whole thing to be angry. "The wolves will not harm the village. Now just come along and show me where you saw the wolf yesterday."

"He is probably still there, waiting to attack us."

He sighed and looked at Pretty Bird.

She said, "I trust Wolf Brother. Besides, Grandfather says we must go. So I am going. If you do not come, you will have to tell him why."

She marched off with her basket. Wolf Brother followed. After a minute, Little Squirrel came trailing behind. Spotted Pony joined them. The four went almost a mile, and then Little Squirrel pointed ahead.

"Look. There is where I dropped my basket."

It was lying on its side, a few berries still within and more spilled on the grass. Just beyond was the berry patch. The ground was covered with thick grass, and even though the boys searched carefully, they were unable to find any tracks. However, Wolf Brother did find a tuft of gray wolf fur caught on some thorns.

"See, I told you," cried Little Squirrel triumphantly, when she saw it in his fingers.

A crooked stick lay on the ground a short distance away. One end of it was freshly splintered, and Wolf Brother picked it up to look at it more closely. There were teeth marks on it, strong punctures and gashes, as though the wolf—or something else with long, sharp teeth—had been furiously chewing on it.

He was puzzled. Why would a wolf, or any other animal, gnaw on a stick? It didn't make any sense at all.

The girls began picking berries. The boys explored around the patch but couldn't find any more sign.

Wolf Brother thought he should go to the wolves, to speak to them and ask what they knew of this strange thing. But the dens were far away, on the other side of the village from where he was now. The hot sun beat down on him. Sweat ran in little rivers down his bare back and chest. He really didn't want to go so far on this hot day for something that probably wasn't important at all.

Spotted Pony seemed to read his mind. "The water will be cool," he said.

Wolf Brother nodded, and they went to the river.

That night he had a dream. He dreamed he was standing in the berry patch. He heard a low, terrible growling and looked up to see several wolves coming toward him. They all carried sticks in their mouths and chewed angrily on them as they trotted along. Wolf Brother called a greeting, but they did not reply. They came closer, and he saw they were looking strangely at him.

Suddenly he was afraid. He knew something was wrong. He began to walk toward the village, and they followed him. He walked faster, and they came faster. He broke into a trot, and they loped along more quickly.

I must get to the village, he thought. The people will save me from the wolves.

But that was silly. No one had to save him from the wolves, for they were his brothers. And now he realized that if he led the wolves into the village while they were snarling and acting

so fierce, they would surely be killed by the people.

He looked over his shoulder and they were close behind him, growling and grinding their teeth on the sticks.

What am I going to do? he wondered. Who am I going to save, the wolves or myself?

Something touched his shoulder and he jumped, thinking one of the wolves had reached him. But it was Aunt Pigeon.

"Wake up," she said. "You are twitching like a dog. You must be having a powerful dream."

He told her what it was.

"Too bad your father just left. When he comes back, you must be sure to tell him. Perhaps he can explain what it means."

It wasn't quite so hot that morning. A few clouds were in the sky, dulling the blazing sun, and a little breeze stirred the air around. Wolf Brother got his pony and rode toward the wolf dens. He was sure something was wrong, and he had to find out what it was.

EIGHT

Halfway between the village and the wolf dens, the trail crossed a stony ridge. As he rode over the top, Wolf Brother saw a movement on the slope below him. He reined in Gisapa.

It was a wolf, and he recognized him as old Lop-Ear, a single male from the far upper end of the valley. At first he thought Lop-Ear was hunting, because he was moving with his nose to the ground. Then he saw that he was only snuffling along, snapping at sticks and stones. He went first in one direction and then another, zig-zagging back and forth.

Lop-Ear howled in an angry, frustrated way. His voice was hoarse and strange. If Wolf Brother had not been looking right at him, he never would have recognized the sound as coming from Lop-Ear but would have thought it the howl of some unknown wolf.

Wolf Brother watched him, wondering what he was doing. Gisapa watched too, shifting his feet uneasily. His hoof struck a rock, which rolled down the hill, banging and clattering over other rocks.

Without even looking to see who or what had made the sound, Lop-Ear charged up the hill. Wolf Brother watched in amazement. Wolves are normally cautious animals, wary and even shy. Now Lop-Ear was attacking blindly, without seeming to know or care what he was after.

He called to him, telling him who he was, but if Lop-Ear heard, he did not pay any attention. He just raced up the hill, all the while staring at Wolf Brother with a terrible intensity.

Gisapa stamped his feet and whirled around. Half rearing, he tossed his head against the pull of the leather thong that circled his lower lip. Wolf Brother checked him, looking over his shoulder.

Lop-Ear was nearly to the top of the ridge. His strong legs carried him swiftly up the slope. Foamy drops of saliva spilled from his open mouth.

He's gone mad! Wolf Brother thought. He loosened the reins, and Gisapa leaped forward. He was in a run in a few steps, and he pounded recklessly down the ridge, back the way he had come. Lop-Ear ran close behind.

They thundered through some bushes in the middle of the little valley. A covey of quail exploded out of the underbrush, scattering wildly in all directions. Without slowing his stride, Lop-Ear veered sharply to the left. Mindlessly, as though he no longer controlled his body, he leaped off in pursuit of the quail. As he disappeared from sight in the bushes, Wolf Brother saw the branches waving back and forth to mark his passage.

He slowed Gisapa to a trot and rode back to the village. Shadow Fox still was not home, and Wolf Brother paced restlessly up and down in front of the lodge.

Little Squirrel came walking by and looked oddly at him. She went into her lodge, and after a minute her mother put her head out and looked at him too. Wolf Brother didn't notice. He walked several paces, turned around, and walked back again.

Come home, Shadow Fox, he said silently. Wherever you are, hear me and come home. I need you now.

Little Squirrel's mother went to Owl Feather's lodge and spoke softly through the door. Owl Feather, his parents, and a sister filed out. They stood watching Wolf Brother.

Wolf Brother stalked a few steps and turned again. Back and forth, he prowled in front of his lodge.

Shadow Fox, hurry.

All at once he was aware that he was being watched. He stopped and saw a dozen people gathered in a silent group, all looking at him. Their faces were unfriendly, their eyes hard and suspicious. He felt fear and dislike coming from them. It flowed toward him, so strong and real it was like a solid force that he could nearly touch. He could almost feel it slamming into him, bruising him, knocking him to the ground.

What is wrong? he wondered. What do they think I have done now?

Should he go into his lodge, or should he stay where he was? He had the feeling that if he moved, they would all scream and come charging at him. A slight trembling began in his knees and moved up his thighs into his stomach and chest. It settled in his heart, which began to thump like a tomtom.

The tall figures of Many Buffalo and the old chief, Black Deer, came shuffling through the middle of the village. They moved slowly and carefully, both lame and stiff with age, both carrying the scars of many battles. Still, they were straight and proud with the dignity of their years and their honorable wounds. They passed in front of the villagers, and their bodies were like shields, deflecting the anger.

The two came to Wolf Brother, and Many Buffalo took him by the arm. "Go into your lodge, Wolf Brother," he said softly.

Wolf Brother slipped inside without a word. The two old warriors sat down, one on each side of the entrance. Their hard, old faces seemed carved out of stone, and their dark eyes stared off into distances that no one else could see.

The other people turned, and one by one they went about their business.

After they were gone, Wolf Brother crawled over to the flap. "What was wrong?" he whispered. "What happened?"

"You were pacing up and down," said Many Buffalo. "Back and forth, back and forth. Wolves pace like that. They are afraid that if you become more wolflike, Looks-Away's dream will come true and you will join with the wolves in destroying the village."

Wolf Brother closed his eyes and slumped over on the

ground. So now they thought he was turning into a wolf. No matter what he did, it was wrong. Even the simplest action, one that would seem ordinary for anyone else, became suspect when he did it.

Black Deer spoke from outside the tent. "No one will harm you now. We will stay here until Shadow Fox comes home."

After a while Aunt Pigeon came in with a basket of roots. She didn't have much to say, and Wolf Brother knew someone had told her what had happened. Several hours passed, in almost total silence. The motionless shadows of the two warriors sitting outside dimmed and merged into the other shadows of the night. It was well after dark before Shadow Fox arrived at last. He spoke softly to the two old men outside before he came into the tipi.

"I was hunting far away and would have stayed out another night," he said. "But then I thought I heard you call my name. I thought I heard you say, 'Shadow Fox, come home.'"

"I did call you," said Wolf Brother. "Something has happened to Lop-Ear." He did not mention the other event. They would talk about that later.

Shadow Fox listened to Wolf Brother's story.

"You are right. Lop-Ear has gone mad. This happens to animals sometimes as well as people."

"What can we do? How can we help him?"

Shadow Fox shook his head. "There is no way we can help him."

"There must be come medicine. You have so many cures and potions."

"There is no medicine against this madness. The animals who have it cannot swallow water. In a few days he will die. I have seen this before, and it is always the same."

Wolf Brother was silent.

"There is danger now from Lop-Ear. You saw how he charged at you. He will attack anything that moves, either animal or human. He has lost all sense of fear and caution and

knows only rage. He might charge into the midst of the village. If he did, everyone would be sure Looks-Away's dream was true. He would be killed. You might be killed too, and I could not save you.

"He might also attack his own kind, the wolves. If he bites anyone, the madness will pass to them and they will die too. We must kill Lop-Ear before he kills someone else. As soon as it is light in the morning, we will go out to hunt him. This is something we must do, and you must understand."

Wolf Brother lay a long time waiting for sleep to come. He thought of Lop-Ear. Was he sleeping or was he out roaming around in the darkness, driven by the unnatural rage that controlled him? What would happen if he came upon Wolf Mother and Wolf Father or Wolf Sister, Blackfoot, and their pups? Lop-Ear might kill them. Even if they survived his attack, they would pass the madness on to each other. If one of his wolf family was bitten, he and Shadow Fox would have to kill that one to keep him from hurting the others. How could he kill one of his own family?

If Lop-Ear did infect the other wolves, maybe they would all go mad. Maybe Looks-Away's dream would come true. Maybe a whole pack of insane wolves, his own wolf family among them, really would attack the village. And if Wolf Brother himself was bitten, would he be among the wolves, ripping and tearing with his teeth at the lodges?

It was all too terrible to think about, and yet he could not stop thinking. He wished the morning would come.

The sun had barely risen when he and Shadow Fox rode out of the village. Wolf Brother was so tired from his almost sleepless night that he could barely move. His head hurt with a dull pain. His fingers were stiff, and there seemed to be a fuzzy veil in front of his eyes. He kept blinking and squinting, trying to make it go away, trying to see clearly.

They rode to the place where Wolf Brother had last seen Lop-Ear, chasing the quail up the little valley. Shadow Fox dismounted and cast around for wolf sign. With difficulty he was able to follow Lop-Ear's trail. He had turned to the left again and recrossed the stony ridge at a point above where he had chased Wolf Brother the day before.

His tracks went down the other side, wandering back and forth without any pattern or sense. Beyond the ridge they found a place where he had lain down for a while. They saw where he had rushed after a rabbit. The rabbit tracks ran along the edge of a little stream, but the wolf's tracks turned sharply away.

"He is now afraid of water, even though his body still needs it," said Shadow Fox.

"He must be suffering," said Wolf Brother.

His father nodded. "It will be kind of us to end his pain."

They were getting close to the den where Wolf Sister and Blackfoot had their puppies. Wolf Brother's heart felt dull and heavy. He wanted to shout at Shadow Fox to hurry, but he knew it took time to follow the tracks. What if they were too late? What if Lop-Ear reached the den before they found him?

The trail entered a broad grassy meadow, and there they lost him. They ranged back and forth but couldn't pick up any sign. The sun was high in the sky, and it was hot. It would soon be midday.

In desperation, Wolf Brother went beyond the edge of the meadow and made a big circle all around it. He crouched close to the ground. His eyes sifted back and forth across the space in front of him, searching for the tiniest trace of the wolf's passing.

All at once he saw two pebbles that had been moved. There were two darker spots where the earth was still a little moist. The sun had not yet dried them to the color of the rest. A few yards beyond, they found a single wolf track in a patch of dust.

"You have good eyes, Wolf Brother. And look, he has turned another way. He is going away from the den."

Wolf Brother felt a little easier, but he knew that Lop-Ear

might turn back again at any time. His head felt better and his vision had cleared. It helped to be out doing something instead of lying in his robes, imagining the worst.

"Father, I want to go to the den and tell the wolves that Lop-Ear is mad. Even if he does not go near the den, they might meet him while they are hunting. If I warn them, they can avoid him."

"Very well. But if you do see Lop-Ear, you must kill him at once. Do not let him get near you. He is no longer friend to anyone."

Wolf Brother lifted his bow. "I know what I must do, and I will do it."

"Good." Shadow Fox put his hand on his shoulder. "After you have talked to the wolves, come after me. I will mark the trail for you to follow."

Wolf Brother nodded. He swung up on Gisapa, who was following along behind with Shadow Fox's horse. Thumping his heels against his ribs, he sent him galloping across the meadow.

NINE

When Wolf Brother got near the den, he called and Wolf Sister answered. He slid off Gisapa and tied him to a tree. Wolf Sister came bounding out to meet him, followed by her fat puppies. She raised up on her hind legs, putting her paws on his chest, and they touched noses. The puppies leaped around him, pulling and chewing on his leggings, and he bent down to greet them.

He told Wolf Sister about Lop-Ear, and she understood at once. Blackfoot was out hunting. They could not warn him until he returned.

She yipped at the puppies, telling them to go back to the den. They were excited at seeing Wolf Brother and would not obey her. Instead, they ran around and around in circles, chasing each other. Wolf Sister was angry and gave one of them a sharp nip on the rump. He yelped and fell over on his back, waving his paws in the air.

Suddenly Lop-Ear came out of the bushes. He walked slowly, with his head down, staggering dizzily from side to side. He growled, low and angrily, as if muttering to himself. Bits of form clung to his muzzle and dripped from his mouth.

One dragging hind foot sent a rock rolling out in front of him. Snarling, he snatched it up and chewed on it. An eye-tooth broke of and dropped to the ground. He seemed not to notice but gulped and swallowed the rock. Blood from his broken tooth turned the form to red.

His glazed eyes focused on the boy and the wolves. The puppies streaked for the den with Wolf Sister right behind them, but Wolf Brother faced him, standing between Lop-Ear and the den.

He fitted an arrow to his bow. Lop-Ear lurched toward him in a stumbling trot. The pupils of his eyes were unnaturally big and dark. He snarled and slobbered, glaring at Wolf Brother with furious eyes.

Wolf Brother aimed carefully, stretching the bow as far as it would go. He held his position steadily, even as the wolf loomed closer. He fired, and the arrow sank deep into Lop-Ear's chest. The wolf cried out and rolled over, snapping at the shaft. He ripped off the feathers with his powerful teeth. Then he stretched out and lay still.

Wolf Brother put another arrow in his bow and waited. When Lop-Ear did not move, he crossed to him. The wolf's eyes were almost closed. He was dead.

Wolf Sister and her puppies came out of the den behind him, just as a wolf howled from a nearby hill. It was Blackfoot, coming home from the hunt. Wolf Sister pointed her nose at the sky and howled back, telling him to come home, telling him his family was safe.

Wolf Brother found Shadow Fox, and they returned together to the place where Lop-Ear's body lay. They searched for a hole in the ground and enlarged it with sharp sticks. Then they put the wolf's body inside and covered it with sand and rocks. He must be deeply buried so no one else would be infected with his madness.

"Come, Wolf Brother," his father said. "We will swim in the river and cool off before we go back to the village."

Wolf Brother hesitated. The water would feel good, but the river was close to the village, a long way from where he was now.

"I am not going back to the village," he said at last. He explained what had happened the day before. "If Black Deer and Many Buffalo had not come when they did, I know the others would have attacked me. They would have chased me out of the village or even killed me. I cannot go back."

Shadow Fox sighed and looked at the sky as though hoping a good omen would appear.

"I will come visit you when times are better," said Wolf Brother. "Tell Aunt Pigeon and Spotted Pony. I hope they will understand."

"Of course they will understand. Wolf Brother, I cannot say, 'Come back with me. Things will be better now,' because I do not think things will be better very soon. It may be that this trouble is a test for you. The spirits do things in ways that we cannot always understand.

"You have a choice that most of us never have to make. You can choose whether you want to live as a wolf or as a human being. But think carefully before you make this decision. You will live the rest of your life either as a man who is part of his band or as a stranger who is always apart from his own kind."

"I do not have to decide," Wolf Brother said. "The people have decided for me. They do not want me, and I will not stay where I am not wanted."

His father looked gravely at him. "If that is how you feel, then that is how it must be. I wish you well, brother of the wolves."

He put one hand on each shoulder and squeezed tightly. Wolf Brother felt his strong fingers pressing into his flesh. He wanted to fling his arms around Shadow Fox's waist and hold on, but he knew if he did he would cry. Instead, he stood stiffly and watched as Shadow Fox vaulted onto his horse's back.

"You can take Gisapa," the boy said. His voice sounded hoarse and strangled, and he cleared his throat. "I will not need him anymore."

Shadow Fox leaned over and took the braided rawhide rope in his hand. The horses whirled together and clattered away over the rocks and sand.

Wolf Brother watched them until they were out of sight. Then he lay down under a little tree in the shade. He was hot

77

and sticky and miserable. The sand felt gritty beneath the bare skin on his shoulders. Maybe he should have called Shadow Fox back, but now it was too late. And he was tired of people disliking him, tired of unfriendly eyes that found fault with everything he did.

Wolf Sister came over to him, wagging her tail. She lay down beside him and began licking his face, washing off the salty tears that ran down his cheeks. The pups came over and lay down too. They were subdued, made quiet by the heat and the death of Lop-Ear and the sorrow they felt in the air. They stretched their soft little bodies around him and fell asleep. Blackfoot was off to one side, head up, panting, watching with his pale, cold eyes.

It was like being back in the den when Wolf Brother was a baby. A feeling of peace, a sense of rightness came over him. He would never have to face hostile eyes again.

Wolf Sister licked on, soothing him. He felt small, as though he were shrinking down to the baby he had been, down to the size of a wolf cub. He closed his eyes. He could almost feel fur growing on his stomach, covering his bare human skin. His fingernails would grow and curl, turning to claws. The palms of his hands and the soles of his feet would thicken, becoming pads. His teeth would lengthen and sharpen in his mouth. His voice would change until the human words were forgotten and he would speak only in the tongue of wolves.

He was with his true family, and if the spirits were kind to him, they would take him back completely. He would become all wolf, as he was meant to be.

Already dreaming, he fell asleep.

When he woke up, he was still human, but it didn't matter. The feeling of peace and rightness remained. The wolves were happy to have him, as always. He could not tell them that this time was different from the others, that this time he had come to stay forever. They did not know the meaning of the word *forever*.

Days passed. Wolf Brother was absorbed into the life of the

pack. He hunted with them, slept with them, took his turn looking after the cubs.

He tried not to think, but to live like the wolves, feeling nothing beyond the sensations of the moment. He concentrated all his thoughts on searching for sign of game, on following the tracks of the animals they hunted. Like the wolves, he was aware of all the tiny changes that took place around him.

His eyes followed the flight of birds and the silvery flutter of leaves turning in the wind. He watched insects moving through their miniature forest of twigs and grass stems. He smelled the sharp scent of sage and the dawn dampness of the earth. He felt the softness of the grass, the prickle of sand and gravel, the rough shapes of rocks and tree bark beneath the palms of his hands.

Sometimes, especially at night, he felt as though he had become almost invisible. His edges blurred and melted, blending into everything else, until he was no longer separate but a part of everything around him. He felt that when he walked, he left no footprints but moved without disturbing the smallest leaf or pebble.

He could pass through trees and come out whole on the other side, but in the moment of passing he became one with the tree. His skin became bark and his arms and legs were the limbs, forever fastened to the earth and yet growing and changing with a whole life of their own.

These special times of complete belonging when he just existed, as clear and empty and unfeeling as running water, were rare. Most of the time he was still Wolf Brother. Most of the time he was content to be with the wolves and live their way of life. It was simple, and though it was hard on his body—he was often tired and sometimes hungry and he knew that in the winter to come he would often be cold—it was easy on his mind. There was no difficult choices to make and no critical eyes waiting to pass judgment on everything he did or said.

Nevertheless, he was sometimes lonely. He missed the life of the village, the sounds of other people, children playing, the soft voices of the women singing as they did their tasks, the deeper murmur of the men. He missed the smoke from the cooking fires and the sound of Aunt Pigeon laughing.

He wrestled and played with the puppies, and he remembered wrestling with Spotted Pony. The puppies were fun, but he could not talk to them as he talked with Spotted Pony. He missed the jokes they had shared and their talk about the brave deeds they would do when they grew up. Now they would grow up separately, and if he did brave deeds, only the wolves would know.

He missed Shadow Fox most of all. It was true he was his adopted father, but he was more than that. He was his guide, his advisor, his bridge between the world of the wolves and the life of the village. Spotted Pony was his good friend, Aunt Pigeon loved him, but no one would ever understand him as Shadow Fox understood him.

Perhaps the bond existed because they were both different. Wolf Brother felt he was different because he was born outside the band. Shadow Fox was born in and was part of the band, but there was a difference in his spirit that set him apart. It was what made him a good medicine man. It was why even people who knew him well, other men who had grown up with him and called him friend, looked at him with respect. It was why he lived without a wife when he was rich enough to have several if he wished. After his second wife died, he said, "I will not marry again. It is the wish of the spirits that I not belong to anyone but them."

Yet he gave himself to Wolf Brother, and in return Wolf Brother had always wanted to do great things that would make Shadow Fox proud. He wanted to justify the medicine man's faith in him and bring honor to his house. Now he never would. No songs would ever be sung about Wolf Brother, recounting the deeds he had done for his tribe. There would be no tales told about him for the ones who came after to hear and remember.

His heart ached as he thought of all his bright dreams that dissolved like rainbows as he tried to reach them. Perhaps it was meant to be. He had never had a history like the other people, and now he was no longer one of them. In time, he would forget the human things that still bothered him, and even if his body stayed human, he would be all wolf inside.

He was hunting with Wolf Father and Wolf Mother, and they came upon a herd of deer feeding together. They crept quietly forward on the downwind side, crawling as close as they dared. An old buck grazed off to the side. One of his legs seemed stiff, and he favored it whenever he took a step. Wolf Father inched closer. The buck was the prey they would go after.

The wolves could not kill a strong young deer in good condition but had to seek out the old or the weak. The deer flung up his head and Wolf Father leaped forward, his mate right behind him. Wolf Brother ran farther behind. He couldn't keep up with the wolves when they were running full speed. Usually they were too impatient to wait and let him get close enough to take a shot with his bow and arrow. They were used to doing things their own way.

The rest of the herd bounded off in another direction. Old and stiff as he was, the buck put on a burst of speed. He leaped and zigzagged through the bushes, bouncing over the tops of some and dodging around others. When he realized that he could not outrun them, the deer stopped in front of thick bushes to protect his flank. He whirled to face the wolves.

They advanced toward him, one on the left and one on the right. The buck raked his antlers back and forth and lashed out with his forefeet. The wolves dodged and lunged in again. Wolf Father was as old and stiff as the deer, and this time he was not quick enough. The sharp hoof caught him in the head, and he fell without a sound.

Wolf Mother continued attacking. Wolf Brother came panting up and fitted an arrow in his bow. He looked at Wolf Father, who was lying on the ground with blood oozing from his wound. He forgot about shooting and ran to the wolf. Wolf Father's skull was crushed. He was already dead.

The deer broke and ran again, with Wolf Mother leaping behind him.

"Come back. Come back," he shouted, but she was intent on the hunt and did not listen.

Wolf Brother sat on the ground, stroking the wolf's fur and remembering, all the hunts, all the days and nights when Wolf Father had stood guard over his family. He remembered his voice calling from the ridge when he brought food to the starving people. He remembered wrestling with the wolf, rolling over and over on the ground, with the mock-fierce growls sounding in his ears. He remembered gazing into his eyes, clear gray with dark slits in the middle, while Wolf Father laughed his wolfish laugh and put his big paws on his knees.

He was still sitting, stroking him, when Wolf Mother came trotting back.

"He is dead," he said. He stood and moved aside.

Wolf Mother whined and crept over to him with her head and tail close to the ground. She sniffed at Wolf Father, and then she lay down and rested her head on the boy's feet.

She is a wolf after all, Wolf Brother told himself later. She is not a woman. It is foolish of me to blame her for acting like a wolf.

And yet he could not forget how Wolf Mother had charged off after the deer, so intent on the thought of food that she did not notice her mate was dead. He told himself that wolves had no time for softness in their lives. They were often hungry and food was too precious to let anything stand in the way of getting it. There was nothing wrong in acting like a wolf if you were a wolf.

Although Wolf Mother did grieve, in the way of wolves, it seemed to Wolf Brother that there should be some ceremony to mark his wolf father's passing. He could not go off and leave him lying on the ground. He lifted his body up into a small

tree, in the way of the Lakota, so his spirit could rise easily into the sky on its way to the afterworld. He sang a song about him, telling what a fine wolf he had been, always brave and faithful, and a good hunter. Then he walked away and left him to the spirits.

TEN

Wolf Brother lay on the hill above the village. He had been there most of the afternoon, watching the activity below. Today was a feast day. Pretty Bird's oldest sister was getting married. All day the smoke from the fires had drifted skyward as the women prepared the wedding banquet.

Pretty Bird's sister came out, dressed in her finest clothes adorned with fringes and porcupine quills. She wore heavy necklaces, bracelets, and earrings. Her hair was braided and decorated with feathers. Even from this high hill, Wolf Brother could see that she was beautiful.

He watched the dancing and the ceremonies, listened to the sounds of chanting and the beating of the drums. Sometimes he could almost hear words as the people shouted back and forth, laughing and joking with each other.

Wolf Mother watched with him for a while, her ears pricked forward, interested in what was going on below. But then she grew bored. She yawned, whined restlessly, and tried to coax Wolf Brother to come hunting with her. When he refused, she curled up with her nose under her tail and napped. When she woke up, she went off hunting without him, unwilling to wait anymore.

Wolf Brother was hungry too. His stomach gnawed on emptiness, and he knew if he waited any longer, he would not eat at all that day. It was nearly too dark for him to see to aim his arrow. The smell of the cooking food drifted to him and made him even hungrier. He thought of roasted meat, crispy brown on the outside and tender juicy within, and his mouth filled with saliva.

There was no point in lying here any longer. The ceremony was over. The drums had been put away. The women escorted the bride to her new lodge, where her husband would join her. The others drifted off to their own lodges. A few sat sleepily by the dying fires, still talking over the events of the day. Gradually they disappeared until no one was left and all the feast fires crumbled into ashes.

Wolf Brother still lay on the hill. He turned over onto his back, and his eyes searched the patterns in the stars above him. He had never felt more alone in his life. He knew he should move farther away from the village while it was still dark. Someone might find him here when morning came.

But he did not want to go. He did not want to lose his physical closeness to the people. He had come nearly every night since Wolf Father died, and he watched from this hill. He crept quietly away as soon as the people went to sleep, carefully erasing his tracks as he went so no one would find out he had been there.

All his relief at escaping to the simple, peaceful wolf life had completely vanished. The death of Wolf Father had destroyed forever his illusion of living like a wolf himself. He could not find food and hunting more important than the loss of a loved one. He could not let death pass unmarked by any ceremony. He needed the singing, the drums, and the ceremonies, the mingling of talk, laughter, and tears that was human life. He was not a wolf and he never would be. He wanted to go home.

But he could not. His pride would not let him be a burden and an embarrassment to Shadow Fox. He would not go back to suffer the unfriendliness of the last few months. He did not want to guard every word and action for fear that he might trigger violence and be driven with sticks and stones from the village.

Neither could he stay where he was, watching the feasting and laughter from shadows, neither wolf nor human, but something trapped in between. He would have to leave entirely, go far away to a new country where no one had ever heard of him at all. Maybe, if he was lucky, another tribe might take him in. He could tell them lies about his family, about his parents and grandparents, his brothers and sisters, and maybe they would believe him. Maybe they would kill him, but it would be better to be dead than not belong anywhere at all.

It was almost morning. He must have slept part of the night without knowing it. He got to his feet and went slowly down the hill. It didn't matter now if he left tracks behind him. He didn't care anymore if everyone knew he came back at night to watch the village.

Wolf Brother started walking south. The Pawnee and the Arapahoe lived in that direction. He had little hope that they would be friendly, but one direction was as good as another.

There was no one to tell good-bye. He had already said good-bye to Shadow Fox, Aunt Pigeon, Spotted Pony, and Many Buffalo as he lay on the hill above the sleeping village. There was nothing to say to them that they did not already know.

Wolf Sister and Blackfoot had each other and their yearly family of cubs. They did not need anyone else.

Wolf Mother would miss him. She would probably follow his trail as she had before when Shadow Fox took him from the den as a baby. But she would not venture far outside her own territory. She had her own place of belonging, with her own family, and she could be killed if she journeyed into the territory of other wolves.

She would follow but she would turn back, and because she was hungry, she would hunt. The hunting would absorb her, take all her time and thoughts. When her stomach was full, she would clean her paws and sleep. When she woke, she would watch birds flying, bugs crawling, smell the rich scents of the earth, feel the warmth of the sun on her fur. She was too busy living to think much about what was lost. She would remember him, but he would fade into the shadowy past, along with Wolf Father.

Wolf Brother was terribly tired. He had jogged and walked for miles, and now his legs were weak, as though they would fold under him at any instant. He wanted to lie down, but not out in the middle of the open plain. He hurried on, and just over the next hill was a little creek. He drank and then lay down to rest in the shade of the willows.

He felt as though he were tearing apart inside. He was leaving behind everything he had known in his entire life, everything that was important to him. Whatever his future might hold, he knew nothing would be harder or hurt more than what he was doing now. Wolf Brother tried to concentrate on the leaves above his head, to let himself be absorbed into the tree, but tears kept getting in the way. His eyes were so blurred he could see nothing at all. His chest and throat ached so much the only thing he could think of was himself.

Wolf Brother must have slept again, because he could tell by the sun that it was late afternoon. He wondered why he fell off to sleep so easily and then realized it had been a long time since he had eaten. He didn't feel hungry, just tired and light-headed.

Maybe I will starve to death, he thought rather giddily. And then I won't have to worry about anything anymore.

He could see the creek from where he lay under the bushes. A little red crawfish worked its way along the bottom, holding its pincers out in front. Wolf Brother crawled down to the bank and reached in after it. The crawfish shot backward, much faster than it had gone forward. It scuttled under a rock, stirring up a little cloud of mud.

Wolf Brother caught it easily by reaching behind its claws. He killed it with a rock and ate it raw. It wasn't very big, but it was something in his stomach. He drank some more water and then started walking along the creek, following its wandering course.

Night came again and he slept. He woke once in the dark and heard a wolf howling. He had never heard its voice before, and he knew he was in the territory of strangers. He rolled over and went back to sleep.

In the morning he caught another crawfish and started walking again. The sun pressed upon him like a giant hand, so hot it felt heavy on his body. Heat waves danced in front of him, blotting out the horizon. Sometimes he couldn't see more than a foot or two in front. The air seemed thick and wavered and shimmered around him. The sensation was like being underwater, though he walked upon dry land. He kept brushing his hands in front of his face, trying to push away the gluey mass, and yet he found nothing there.

Sometimes, as though looking out through a doorway, he could see hills and grassy plains in the distance. They were perfectly still, each grass blade clear and distinct, as though each one had been carefully drawn with a sharp knife upon stone. It was as though no wind had ever blown through that petrified landscape. It must have existed since back before the creation, even before the spirits moved upon the earth.

There was no life in that grass. Each blade was as unmoving as rock. The doorway got wider, opening before him. Wolf Brother kept walking toward it, clumping along on feet of stone, toward the stone grass. And then he was through the doorway and inside. The grass was very tall and brown all around him. It was higher than his head, and he was like a little insect moving in it. He was the only thing that had ever moved through that thousand-year-old wasteland of grass as tall as trees.

Wolf Brother trembled at the thought. What was he doing here? What right did he have to be bumbling along, disturbing the thousand-year silence? He stopped, and for one long moment he was as still as the grass itself.

And then the grass moved, just the tips at first. Gently it inclined toward the ground, as though each blade bent its head to listen. And something was coming. At first it was so far away that he could barely hear it: only a tiny murmur, far off

at the edge of sound. It came closer, growing steadily into a roar, a mighty *whooshing* that bent each blade of grass until it was flat to the earth.

The wind was blowing. Wolf Brother seemed to be the only thing that wasn't touched by this vast, howling gale that leveled everything upon the earth as it went beating by. The air whirled around him with a terrible wailing, but he was untouched.

With the wind came darkness. Something moved behind the darkness, something he felt but could not see. Wolf Brother fell down upon the ground, as flat as the grass had been.

"Oh, Great Spirit," he cried. "Have pity upon me."

"Wolf Brother, I come to help you," a voice said. And the roaring stopped.

The wind still blew, but in silence. Now Wolf Brother could feel the air passing around him, moving his clothing, his hair. It was strong, but no longer a gale. The grass had shrunk back to normal size and waved gently at his feet.

He could hear a song. It seemed to come from the earth and the grass and the sky and the four winds and from within himself. He had never heard it before, and yet it was so familiar he wondered why he had never thought of it himself. The song expressed everything he felt and told him things he had never known. It was so special and so true that he knew at once it was for him alone. It would always be his song.

Then he seemed to be standing near his village. He could see the whole tribe—Aunt Pigeon, Spotted Pony, Many Buffalo, Looks-Away, and the rest—standing in front of their lodges. Shadow Fox was there, slightly off to one side.

The wind blew from behind him, and he felt something else there too. He turned and saw a tall figure, half in darkness, half in light. It changed and shifted as he looked at it. Sometimes it seemed to be a tall and noble warrior, who looked at him with dark, distant eyes. Sometimes it seemed the shape of a great wolf. And sometimes it was something else entirely.

A current flowed from the being into him. He felt it passing through his body, strong and pulsing. It flowed from him toward the villagers, and they lifted their hands to receive it. Then the current changed. It reversed itself and flowed from the people into him, passing through his body to the spirit behind him.

He felt pressure from another direction and saw the wolves sitting off to his right. A pulsing came from them too. All the feelings, wolf and human, joined into a great river running through him. They mingled together, joy and sadness, fear and comfort, need and fulfillment. As the shifting currents passed through him, he felt himself filling with strength and resolution, as a vessel is filled when water pours into it.

Wolf Brother looked off beyond the lodges and saw herds of horses and buffalo moving along the horizon, passing by the village. He raised his hands and beckoned. They turned and came toward him, coming to his hand with a great rumbling and cloud of dust.

He closed his eyes as they surrounded him. He would feel the solid shapes passing around him, barely brushing against his arms. The ground vibrated with their many hooves. He smelled the odors of sweat and animal hide, and the thick dust clogged his nostrils.

When they were gone, he opened his eyes. He was lying on ordinary grass beside the banks of the stream he had followed all day. Water flowed by with a silvery gurgle, dappled with shade from the leaves of the willows that moved in the gentle breeze. A haze of clouds slipped between the earth and the sun, softening the pressure of the burning rays.

Wolf Brother rubbed his hands over his eyes and sat up groggily.

I have had my dream, he thought in wonder. I have received my vision. But how could it happen? I did not prepare myself. I am too young and not ready.

He rolled down to the creek and fell into the water, trying to rinse away the dream, to splash himself back to wakefulness and reality. But when he came out, dripping wet, the memory of the dream was still there, as clear and sharp as ever.

He had dreamed. He had not sought his vision, but it had come to him. Whether he was ready or not, it was his. And the message was plain.

He started back toward the village.

ELEVEN

Wolf Brother hadn't gone very far when he met Wolf Mother, trotting along with her nose to the ground, following his trail. He was very glad to see her. By now he was so weak that he could barely walk. He lay down on the creek bank while she hunted.

He was grateful to her for caring about him, for always being faithful. Wolf Brother told her so when she came back, and she was pleased, although she was only doing what she wanted to do.

When he had eaten, he was able to go on. Wolf Mother went with him until they were close to her den, and then she turned off to go to it. She was satisfied now that she had him back where she thought he belonged, in her home territory. Wolf Brother kept walking and reached his village by midafternoon. He heard the camp dogs barking as he drew near.

Two warriors came out to see who was coming. He heard them shouting to the others, and soon everyone was standing in a group, talking together and pointing at him. They grew silent as he approached.

The scene was familiar to Wolf Brother. Everyone gathered together, facing him, keeping him outside. He wondered if it would ever be any different.

Aunt Pigeon started to leave the circle and run toward him, but Crooked Leg and another brave stopped her. Looks-Away stepped forward.

"Come no closer, Wolf Brother," he shouted. "You are not welcome here."

Wolf Brother kept walking.

"This is no longer your village," Looks-Away continued. "We do not want you." His voice became shriller as Wolf Brother paid no attention to him. "Go back!"

Owl Feather ran out to stand beside him. "Go back. Go back," he shouted too.

Looks-Away picked up a rock, and a few others did the same. Wolf Brother prayed they would not stone him before he had a chance to speak. His legs shook with fear and exhaustion, and he was weak from many days without much food. He hoped he would not faint.

Shadow Fox came through the crowd, followed by Many Buffalo, Black Deer, Buffalo Calf, and Spotted Pony. Wolf Brother's spirits rose a little.

They are still with me, he thought. There is still hope.

Buffalo Calf, the chief, raised his hand and the people were quiet. "I give you greetings, Wolf Brother," he said. "We did not expect you to return."

"I did not expect to return," said Wolf Brother. His voice sounded faint and scratchy, not at all the way he wanted to speak at what was one of the most important moments of his life.

He stood quietly, gathering himself together. He summoned up the memory of the powerful spirit who had come riding on the wind, down all the days from ancient times. He remembered the voice that had said, "Wolf Brother, I come to help you." He sang a little of his song and felt an answer come from the earth, the sky, and the four winds, as well as within himself. He felt the power surround him like a shield. As long as that spirit was with him, he could be sure of himself.

"I thought I had left the village forever," Wolf Brother went on. Now his voice was clear and steady with the strength he felt flowing within. "I had no wish to stay where I was not wanted, with people who did not count me as a member of their band. I found I could not live as a wolf either, so I decided to go far away, even though my heart was not in it. Either I would find another tribe or I would die. I did not really care. But before I had gone far, I had a dream. My vision came to me before I sought it, before I was ready. And the dream told me to come back here."

"A vision!" Looks-Away's voice was scornful. "You are too young to have any important dreams."

"He is lying," said Owl Feather. He threw his rock, but it whizzed harmlessly past Wolf Brother's head.

The other people did not move. A young man's vision was so important that they felt even Wolf Brother would not lie about it. If anyone did lie about his vision, the spirits would surely punish him and he would be exposed as a fake.

They looked toward Shadow Fox, who was, first of all, the medicine man and would know about such things. He was standing a little to one side, as he had in Wolf Brother's vision.

"It is unusual to receive your dream when you are so young," he said. "But perhaps you have been preparing yourself. Perhaps you were more ready than you thought. You have been living apart from other people. You probably have been thinking, praying, asking for the direction your life should take. Perhaps, if the hunting was not good, you have even been fasting."

Wolf Brother nodded.

"Then the spirits recognized your need, and they sent your vision now, when you need it. The spirits have spoken."

"You are his adopted father," said Crooked Leg. "Of course you will believe him. Wolf Brother must tell his dream so we can all judge if it is true or not."

"Yes, tell us your dream," said Looks-Away.

Wolf Brother shook his head. "I cannot tell the dream."

"Then you must go," said another warrior.

The people murmured together.

"I will tell you one thing," said Wolf Brother. "If I stay, I will bring you many buffalo and many horses."

Crooked Leg laughed harshly. "We have hardly seen a buffalo all summer."

"It will be easy to judge," said one of the old men. "If he stays and brings the horses and the buffalo, then his vision was true. If he stays and they do not come, then we will know his vision was false."

The people nodded in agreement.

"But not in the village," said Crooked Leg. "It is not right that he should leave and come back as he chooses. He is not yet one of us. And if his vision should prove false, he must leave the village and never come back, as long as he may live."

So it was agreed that Wolf Brother could stay, but not in his own lodge. He built a small wickiup of brush a short distance away from the other lodges, and he spent all his time there. He was not allowed to come into the village, and no one could go out to talk to him. Aunt Pigeon came twice a day to bring him food, but that was all. Even Shadow Fox did not come. Wolf Brother understood that his absence was not because he did not want to talk to him, but because he was trying to be impartial. He was trying to be fair to the tribe as well as to Wolf Brother.

At first Wolf Brother did not mind being alone. It was good to be close to the village again. He was weak from his days with little food and exhausted from his long nights spent watching the village and worrying about what he was going to do. He was content just to sleep and sit in the shade and eat the good food Aunt Pigeon brought him.

Days passed and nothing happened. His strength came back, and he began to be bored and restless. He wandered into the edge of the village but was chased back. Every morning he searched the line of the horizon, looking for the horses and the buffalo that the spirit had promised him, but the prairie stayed empty.

He wasn't the only one looking. It was autumn and time for the fall buffalo hunt, but there were no buffalo. In all the years before, there had always been plenty, but this year they could

not be found. The scouts roamed far and wide, but they came back without sighting the great herds that sometimes darkened the prairie. Without the buffalo, the people could not live through the winter.

Buffalo were killed occasionally as they were needed for food during the spring and summer, but autumn was the time of the big hunt. When a herd was sighted, the whole village went out—hunters, old men, women, children, dogs, and horses.

Now in these empty, anxious days, Wolf Brother remembered past years filled with excitement as the people prepared for the coming winter. He sat by himself, looking toward the quiet village. Other autumns had been filled with dust, cries, wheeling horses, and the lumbering of the huge brown beasts. Now the hubbub and activity was missing.

A favorite method of killing the buffalo was called the "surround." Groups of hunters approached the herd from all sides. Gradually they drove the buffalo into the middle. When they were all collected in a bunch, the hunters started the buffalo running in a circle. The animals ran around and around within the ring of whooping, arrow-shooting warriors. One by one, they fell with arrows in them. Other hunters waited outside the circle, ready to pick off any who might dodge through the ring and try to escape.

When the men had killed as many buffalo as they needed, the women began their work. They skinned them and cut them up. They prepared the meat for drying and the hides for lodges, robes, shields, and clothing. The people used nearly every scrap of meat, sinew, hide, and horn. Almost nothing was wasted.

The only things they left behind on the plains were some of the hearts of the buffalo. They believed the mystic power of these hearts would replace the slain buffalo and an equal number would come back to take the place of those killed for food.

Wolf Brother prowled restlessly around the edge of the

village, ignoring anyone who might be watching. No matter what they thought, he could not sit still. He did not have Gisapa back, and so he walked, looking for some sign of buffalo. It seemed hopeless. The scouts on horseback could go much farther and faster than he could, and yet he had to do something.

The people moved their camp from place to place, hopefully following the scouts. Wolf Brother trailed along behind, even more ignored than the camp dogs. Looks-Away seemed to be everywhere at once. He was always talking, making motions with his long, thin hands, jerking his head so his untidy hair twitched about his shoulders. It seemed to Wolf Brother that his wandering eye had permanently fixed itself upon him. It followed him all the time, full of hatred and a hungry triumph that grew stronger every day.

Several times a day Wolf Brother prayed to the spirit, asking him to remember his promise. He made what poor offerings he could, although he didn't have much to give. The spirit made no reply, and Wolf Brother was filled with despair.

Has he forgotten me? Have I done something wrong? Did I misunderstand?

He longed to talk to Shadow Fox, but the medicine man was busy, making his own sacrifices and incantations, trying to summon the buffalo. He must have known Wolf Brother's need, but he did not respond.

It is all up to me, Wolf Brother thought. But what can I do?

He could not sleep, so he left his little brush hut and walked out onto the prairie. He thought about calling the wolves, to join in their hunt, but was too discouraged. He sat on a rock with his chin in his hands.

The moon was coming full, and the rolling hills were filled with light. He heard a tiny rustling in the grass nearby and knew a little mouse was cautiously venturing out. The sky was empty of clouds, a vast, faintly luminous bowl that curved over the darker earth. There were only a few stars, and they were dim and scattered.

He heard a wolf howling, far away in the distance. It was one of his younger brothers, a son of Wolf Mother, who had gone off to find a territory of his own. Blackfoot answered from somewhere off to the left.

The two wolves talked back and forth, and Wolf Brother listened. The other wolf said there were strangers in his territory, two-legged creatures who had been there the year before. Wolf Brother's heart began to pound. Could the Assiniboin raiders have come back?

He got to his feet and began to trot across the moonwashed prairie, heading toward the place where the wolf had said the strangers were camped. He traveled the rest of the night, and it was dawn when he approached their campsite.

It was an area he knew well. His own band had camped there more than once, in happier times, and he and the other boys had explored every inch of it.

The camp was pitched on high ground above the banks of a creek. Cautiously he got down on his stomach and crawled up to where he could see. The strangers did not seem prosperous. The lodges were small, poor, and tattered. The picket line was off to the left, holding scrawny, starved-looking ponies. One of them was a brown-and-white pinto with a perfect star on his forehead. Wolf Brother recognized the animal. It had once belonged to Shadow Fox and was one of the horses stolen when the camp was attacked the year before. The raiders were back.

Wolf Brother watched until the Assiniboin were up and about. They looked thin and hard and scruffy, like their horses and their tipis. There were only a few women and children. Most of them were tough-looking braves. Even from where he lay, he could see many of them were marked with the scars of old battle wounds.

He crawled off to a safe distance where he ate some dried buffalo meat that he carried with him. As he chewed on the tough jerky, he thought about what he wanted to do. It was dangerous, but he would have to take the chance.

His vision spirit had promised to help him, but he was sure

the spirit also expected him to help himself. He could very well sit at the edge of the village until he was an old man, and no buffalo and no horses would come. Wolf Brother would have to seek them out himself.

He trotted down the creek and climbed a steep, rocky ridge on the other side. Then he put back his head and howled, once more asking Wolf Mother, Wolf Sister, and Blackfoot to come to him. No one answered. He was still too far away for them to hear him.

Wolf Brother ran farther on down the ridge, panting and sweating. He wished he had Gisapa. After about a mile, he tried again. He was out of breath and puffing, so his cry came out wavering and garbled. He waited until his breathing had slowed down and tried once more.

This time Wolf Sister answered, from so far away he could barely hear her. They had just completed their hunt and had to take food to the cubs, but they would come that night.

Wolf Brother was satisfied. He climbed back down the ridge, found a cozy hidden spot by the creek, curled up, and went to sleep.

It was well into the next night before the wolves arrived. First they greeted each other. Then Wolf Brother told them what he wanted to do, including an emergency plan if they were discovered, and the wolves agreed to help.

They did not like strangers in their territory. They had reached a sometimes uneasy peace with the people from Wolf Brother's village, and the wolves and the human beings left each other alone. But other people were different. The wolves didn't know what they might do. Already they had invaded their hunting grounds. They just might decide to shoot one of the wolves for the skin or to use the teeth and claws for necklaces. If the wolves could make them go away, they would be happy to do so.

Blackfoot and Wolf Mother waited down by the creek while Wolf Brother and Wolf Sister crawled up to the Assiniboins' camp. Even though they were sure the people would be asleep by now, they moved as quietly as shadows. Not a twig cracked, not a leaf rustled as they made their approach.

Since they expected everyone to be in their lodges, they were surprised to see a tall shadow moving up and down between the tipis. One of the braves was still up. He paced slowly back and forth, his head down, dragging his feet as though he were tired. After a while he sat down and humped his arms and head over his knees as if he might doze off. He was facing the direction of the horses, and all he had to do was raise his head and open his eyes to see them.

Wolf Brother shifted slightly, easing his cramped muscles. Wolf Sister lay with her chin on her paws and her eyes on the sentry. Several more minutes passed, and Wolf Brother was sure the man had dozed off. Just then the guard gave an abrupt jerk and stood up. He began walking briskly back and forth.

Wolf Brother wondered if he should have Blackfoot come up from the creek and show himself to the warrior. Perhaps he would follow the wolf away from camp. But he might shout instead and wake up the rest of the Assiniboins.

He sighed a little and looked at Wolf Sister, who hadn't moved at all. She was so patient. He would try to be the same.

TWELVE

The night passed slowly, endless dark minutes inching one after another. At last a sort of numbness came over Wolf Brother, and he was able to lie as quietly as the wolf beside him. Perhaps he dozed a little.

It was no longer as dark. The light was turning pale and gray. Wolf Brother did not want to wait for another night. Probably another sentry would be on duty then too. The guard was sitting down again, slumped against a tree. The ragged tipis were like dim stone monuments in the growing light. The horses in the picket line shifted, as though a wind had blown across them. The guard did not stir.

Wolf Brother edged forward stiffly. Wolf Sister stayed where she was. If she went in closer, her wolf scent might disturb the horses. Slowly, carefully, pressing his body flat against the ground, Wolf Brother wiggled like a snake toward the picket line.

When he had almost reached it, one of the horses saw him. He snorted and jerked his head. All the horses shifted back and forth. The noise woke the guard by the fire. He got up and walked toward the tethered horses, holding his lance in his hand. Wolf Brother made himself as small and flat as possible, trying to dissolve into the earth.

The sentry paused and his keen eyes swept back and forth. He saw a small hump on the ground that he didn't remember seeing before. He moved slowly forward, lifting his lance.

Wolf Brother knew he was discovered. He leaped to his feet and hurtled toward the sheltering bushes. The man yelled and charged after him. Wolf Sister shot from her hiding place. Swift and silent, like a gray ghost in the gray light, she streaked toward the sentry. She came from the side, and he didn't see her at all. Eighty pounds of hard, muscular body leaped straight at him and landed on his back and shoulder. She knocked him off his feet, and he sprawled on the ground, dropping his spear.

His yelling awoke the other warriors, and they charged out of the tipis like hornets out of their nests. They saw the boy and the wolf running down the hill. Some raced after him on foot, while others flung themselves on the backs of their horses. Whooping and screeching, they streamed down the hill.

The boy and the wolf vanished into the brush along the creek. A moment later two figures emerged from the bushes on the other side and went leaping up the bank. But they were not a boy and a wolf. The same pale-gray wolf was there, but at her side ran another one, a much larger, more powerful beast. Flickering like shadows in the dawn light, the two wolves streaked away toward the distant hills.

The warriors splashed into the water, their horses' hooves churning it brown and muddy. They charged up and down the creek in both directions. Trackers raced along the banks on both sides, looking for footprints coming out of the water. There were none, except for the two wolves. They could see far down the long creek bank in both directions but found nothing there, nothing but grass and bushes, behind which they had already searched.

The warriors gathered in the middle of the ford and sat in a puzzled silence.

"The boy is not by the creek," one tracker said. "If he were, we would have found him."

"There was a wolf with him," said someone else.

The man who had been sentry shifted uneasily on his horse. "When I chased the boy, the wolf leaped on me from behind. She protected him as though he were her own cub."

105

Another man spoke, "Remember last year when we were here and I was scouting? I told you I saw a boy running with a pack of wolves. I heard them howling back and forth and could not tell by the sound which was wolf and which was boy."

"There is something mysterious here," said an old warrior. "A boy and a wolf ran into the bushes and two wolves ran out. It must mean the boy changed into a wolf and has gone off into the hills. I have heard of such enchantments."

They all looked at one another. The first rays of the sun came over the eastern hills. At the same time they heard two sharp yelps. When they looked up, they saw the two wolves sitting on a near ridge, outlined in black against the glowing sky. The big wolf flung back his head and made a high yapping noise that sounded like laughter.

"He is laughing at us," said one of the warriors.

"He might come back tonight and steal our horses. Or he might bring a great wolf pack with him and kill us while we are sleeping."

"We must not let him creep up on us when we do not know he is coming. We must not let the wolf boy laugh at us. Whether he is boy or wolf, he can be killed."

Yelling to give themselves courage, they sent their ponies lunging through the water and up the bank. The two wolves watched as, the riders pounded across the valley. Just before they started up the ridge, the wolves turned and slipped down the other side.

When Wolf Brother plunged through the bushes and into the creek, Blackfoot and Wolf Mother were waiting for him at the edge of the water. Blackfoot and Wolf Sister splashed across the creek and climbed the bank on the other side. Wolf Brother and Wolf Mother waded upstream along the bank closest to the camp.

Almost immediately the water deepened so the wolf had to swim. In a moment they were at a place that looked no different from any other part of the bank. But there was a difference.

They pushed against the long, coarse grass that hung down

over the pool. The thick, fibrous leaves parted scratchily. They passed through the grass and were inside a low, dark cave. Wolf Brother's head nearly brushed the earth above him when he crouched on the sloping creek bottom. The water lapped around his chin, but there was room enough for him to breathe. He had found this secret place long ago when he played hide-and-seek with the other boys from the village.

He put his arm around Wolf Mother's neck, and they huddled together, barely breathing, while the raiders stormed up and down the creek. Feet pounded on the earth directly above them as the trackers ran up and down. Through the grass screen, they caught glimpses of the bodies of horses and the bare, brown legs of the riders moving back and forth. The muddy water slapped up and down, sometimes covering their noses for a moment.

They heard the muttering of the men's voices as they talked in the middle of the stream, then the two yelps from the wolves upon the ridge. The riders yelled and rushed off in pursuit. A final wash of muddy water slopped over Wolf Brother's nose and settled down. Everything was quiet again.

Still the two of them waited, in case some of the people from camp had come down to watch the chase. Minutes passed, and then Wolf Mother stuck her nose carefully out of the grass and sniffed around. She went out with Wolf Brother behind her.

Quietly they crawled up the bank and wiggled through the bushes toward the camp. Because of the slope of the hill to the creek, they were invisible from the tipis most of the way. They peeked through some tall grass and saw the picket line and the backs of the horses not far off.

Wolf Brother could see three women in the camp, busy over cooking fires. The smoke rose straight up in tall, wavering, white strands, like thick pieces of fraying rope. Two boys about his own age were wrestling beyond the fire. Otherwise, no one was in sight.

He signed Wolf Mother to stay where she was and crept

toward the picket line. The brown-and-white pinto, Star, was at the end of the line. He heard Wolf Brother coming and turned his head toward him, pricking his ears in curiosity. Wolf Brother lay still and gave the little whistle that Shadow Fox always used to call his horses. Star whinnied softly and stamped his foot.

Wolf Brother crawled to the horse's neck and stood up beside him, stroking him on his neck and shoulder. Star seemed glad to see him. His once-sleek coat was rough and patchy, and his bones nearly thrust out through his hide. There were marks on his side and shoulder as though he had been beaten. He was not treated nearly as well by the raiders as he had been by Shadow Fox.

Wolf Brother went quickly down the line, releasing the horses. He had just untied the last one when one of the boys looked toward him and yelled.

He ran back to Star, whom he had left tied. Both boys and the women were screaming and pointing at him. Two braves ran out of a tipi. Not all of them had gone after all. They came tearing toward Wolf Brother, both of them raising their lances.

He loosened the rawhide thong and grabbed Star's long mane with one hand. Then he swung himself up so his leg was over the horse's back. Another quick pull and he was astride, his knees clamped tight around the horse's ribs.

Wolf Mother came bounding out of the bushes, growling and yelping. She rushed at the horses and they whirled, stampeding off toward the creek. Star leaped into a run behind them. The warriors threw their lances. One passed just over Wolf Brother's head as he ducked low on the horse's back. The other thudded into the ground beside him. They thundered down the hill and plunged into the water.

As they climbed the bank on the far side, Wolf Brother saw the remaining Assiniboin standing in front of their lodges, looking after him with helpless fury. He threw back his head and laughed. Without horses they would never catch him.

The horses galloped down the creek, running in the opposite direction from his village. Star flew along behind them. Wolf Mother ran with them for a while, but then she stopped and gave a short howl. She was tired of running around. Wolf Brother didn't need her anymore, and she was going home to her den. Wolf Brother yelped in farewell. He would see her again soon.

Now he had to catch the horses and get them headed the right way. They raced on, manes and tails flying, wild and excited at being able to run free. At last Wolf Brother was able to pass the lead horse and turn him in the direction of the Lakota village.

There was a high ridge in front of them. The horses slowed to a walk and plodded slowly up it, sweating lightly in the warm autumn sun. Star lunged the last few steps to the top. All the horses paused to rest.

Wolf Brother looked off to the northwest. A hawk sailed by overhead, his piercing cry thin and lonely in the air. Below, the long prairie grasses rippled like water in the wind.

Something else moved there, dark and cumbersome, huge shapes that from this distance looked like lumpy stones. Buffalo! Hundreds of them dotted the plain before him, grazing peacefully on the tall grass. The buffalo had come.

Wolf Brother kicked Star in the ribs and drove the loose ponies toward home. It was miles away, and all the horses were lathered as he galloped into the village. The people had heard them coming, and they were all standing outside. Star jolted to a stop, and in the little silence that followed Wolf Brother looked down at his people. Before he spoke, he waited to hear what they would say.

"He has brought back our horses," said Many Buffalo.

He looked at Shadow Fox, and his father was smiling. He could see the pride shining in his eyes as he said, "My son has brought back the horses to his people. His vision was true."

Later Wolf Brother would tell them about the raiders who were almost helpless with most of their mounts gone. Now something else was more important.

"I bring more than horses," said Wolf Brother. "The buffalo have come back. I can show you where they are."

A great cry rose from the village. "Show us where they are," shouted the hunters. "Lead us to the buffalo. Wolf Brother will lead us to the buffalo."

They reached out to touch him, praising him, thanking him for the horses and the buffalo. They surrounded him, gathering him in, taking him to their midst. For the first time, Wolf Brother was drawn into the heart of the village. His acceptance was as good as he had always known it would be.

Over their heads, he saw Looks-Away standing alone. He looked thin and shrunken, like an old man instead of a boy of fifteen. He flinched and lowered his head when Wolf Brother met his eyes.

Looks-Away, I have beaten you forever, thought Wolf Brother. Still, I pity you. You will not have an easy life. And even though you were my enemy, I will not be yours. Someday you may realize that. Or perhaps not. No man can have everyone as a friend.

Spotted Pony came toward Wolf Brother, leading Gisapa so he would have a fresh horse for the ride back to the buffalo. Wolf Brother smiled and clasped his shoulder. To balance his enemy, he had one true friend who had never deserted him.

Wolf Brother knew it no longer mattered that his origins were shrouded in mystery. After all he had done today, no one could ever again say that he was bad medicine for the band.

And just as important as the way the band felt about him was the way he felt about himself. He knew who he was. He was Wolf Brother of the Lakota, son of Shadow Fox, brother of wolves. He would make his own history, and in years to come old men would tell it around the campfires to the children.

He had already begun.

About the Author

Jean Thompson was born in Pontiac, Illinois, but grew up on an isolated ranch without plumbing or electricity in western Oregon. By the time she was twelve, she was helping her father break and train horses.

Mrs. Thompson's husband is a professional forester, and they have lived in Oregon, California, Idaho, Washington, D.C., Alaska, and now Colorado. The Thompsons have two children, and the whole family enjoys hiking and camping in wilderness areas.

About the Artist

Steve Marchesi was born in Astoria, New York, where he still lives, and was graduated from Pratt Institute in 1973. Since then he has worked as a free-lance illustrator.

The black-and-white illustrations for *Brother of the Wolves* were drawn in pencil.